"May I?" Rider asked, offering his arm grandly, as if he were a prince and she were his princess.

Patricia took one last glance around—just to make sure Evan wasn't there. No luck. Where was he anyway? He must have really been upset not to show up for her game at all. *Maybe I should call him,* she thought. *Maybe I should find out how he's doing.*

"Patricia?"

She looked into Rider's blue eyes. He was there for her. He was happy for her. She had been there for Evan earlier that afternoon, but he wasn't here for her now. And here was this guy— this gorgeous, coveted, incredibly available guy, and he was *waiting* for *her.*

Patricia wrapped her arm around Rider's, pulled the band from her ponytail so that her hair would cover the sweaty strands stuck to her neck, and took a deep breath.

"Let's do it," she said.

While You Were Gone

KIERAN SCOTT

BANTAM BOOKS
NEW YORK · TORONTO · LONDON · SYDNEY · AUCKLAND

RL 6, age 12 and up

WHILE YOU WERE GONE
A Bantam Book / May 1999

Cover photography by Michael Segal.

Produced by 17th Street Productions,
a division of Daniel Weiss Associates, Inc.
33 West 17th Street, New York, NY 10011.

ISBN: 0-553-49277-2

Published simultaneously in the United States and Canada

Bantam Books are published by Bantam Books, a division of Random
House, Inc. Its trademark, consisting of the words "Bantam Books" and
the portrayal of a rooster, is Registered in U.S. Patent and Trademark
Office and in other countries. Marca Registrada. Bantam Books, 1540
Broadway, New York, New York 10036.

PRINTED IN THE UNITED STATES OF AMERICA

OPM   0 9 8 7 6 5 4 3 2 1

For my first love

ONE

EVAN SCHNURE WAS obviously insane. This was something Patricia had come to tell herself at least once a day, every day, as kind of a joke. But now she knew for sure. Her boyfriend was just one inning short of a ball game.

"C'mon, Patricia," Evan said. "I do it all the time."

"Are you serious?" Patricia asked. He *couldn't* be serious. She glanced at Evan, then up toward the roof of Jamesport High School, then back at Evan again. He grinned at her. And of course she couldn't help smiling back. When Evan was around, Patricia seemed to lose all control over her cheek and mouth muscles.

"Just give it a try," Evan persisted. "You're an athletic girl." He walked up next to her, nudging her arm with his elbow.

"I play *softball*," she said. "And not very well.

That doesn't mean I can climb a flat brick wall."

"Always underestimating yourself," Evan joked. He had her on that one. Patricia was constantly convinced she couldn't do stuff and then finding out she wasn't that bad—like when she first tried cooking and the meat loaf came out edible, and when she joined the choir and discovered she could actually sing. Plus she *was* the only sophomore pitcher who ever got to play. But still, she'd been keenly aware of her poor climbing skills ever since she'd fallen out of a tree at camp in second grade and broken her arm in three places. Tarzan, she was not. She wasn't even Jane.

Patricia stepped closer to the wall in question and laid one hand against the cool, grainy surface. As she looked up, a warm November-in-Florida breeze whipped her long blond hair around her shoulders. She tucked her hair behind her ears and sighed. Climbing the gym wall to sit on top of the school and watch the sun set was not the type of thing Patricia Carpenter did. But as Evan came up behind her and rested his hands on her waist for support, she knew she was going to do it. Who wouldn't do this for him? Those clear green eyes, that soft, curly brown hair—

"Okay, put your foot in that first hole," Evan said, his mouth close to her ear. She loved his deep, raspy voice. His breath tickled her neck, and the whole left side of her body was suddenly pleasantly warm. "Don't worry. I've got you," he told her.

Patricia nodded and swallowed hard, willing her

2

hands to stop shaking. She *so* didn't want him to see how nervous she was. She put her foot in the brick-size hole. There were open spaces like this all over the wall. Patricia had always seen the missing bricks as some kind of misguided attempt at modern design. Evan, apparently, had always seen them as a ladder.

"Now find a grip," Evan instructed. "Above you to your right."

Patricia slid her arm up until she found the hole and held on, pressing her fingers into the brick. Her hands were sweating, and as Patricia pulled herself up, she scraped her knee on the wall and winced.

"Oh! Watch the knees!" Evan exclaimed.

"Good timing," she said, clenching her teeth. Patricia pushed the pain aside and started to climb. It was slow going and totally awkward, but Evan called out encouragement as she went. A line of sweat soon popped up above her lip, and her underarms started to itch. Great. By the time she got up there, she was going to be soaked *and* smelly. And she was acutely aware of Evan's eyes on her—all she could think about was the fact that she was splayed against a brick wall like Spider-Man gone graceless. She wondered what her butt looked like from that angle.

When Patricia got to the top, she had to use every muscle in her arms to pull herself up onto the white, gravelly roof. Suddenly the long, Coach Cortez-enforced hours in the weight room seemed

3

like a blessing. She turned herself awkwardly and sat down hard.

"Just like a pro!" Evan called up to her.

Patricia studied the throbbing indentations in her reddened hands. "This better be one seriously life-altering sunset!" she called. But there was no need to yell. It only took Evan about five seconds to scale the wall, and he was now settling himself gracefully next to her, so close that their shoulders touched.

"Oh, it is," he said with a little bobbing nod. "A sunset like this one is what inspired me to call you that first time."

Patricia forgot all about her palms. The little heart flop was too distracting. "Aw, isn't that special?" she teased lightly.

"I know. I'm so romantic, it's vomit inducing," he responded.

"I barf every time I kiss you," Patricia joked, nudging him with her shoulder.

"Cool! Can I see?" He leaned over and kissed her before she even had a chance to catch her breath. His lips were soft and warm, and he tasted like cinnamon gum. Patricia's blood raced in her veins.

When he pulled away, she had to ask, "Hey! What happened to the spearmint?"

"I switched," Evan answered, pulling a fresh pack of Trident out of his pocket. The boy was never without gum. "What happened to the barf?"

"Sorry to disappoint." Patricia shrugged and

shook her head sadly. "I guess your ick factor is waning."

"Must do something about that." Evan moved over and sat behind her, wrapping his arms around her and pulling her back, close to his chest. "Maybe I should not shower for a week or something."

Patricia cuddled greedily into his embrace, enveloping herself in his warmth. "Then we probably wouldn't sit like this very often," she told him. Nuzzling his neck, Patricia inhaled his familiar scent of fabric softener and paint thinner. "I love the way you smell."

"Okay. I'll rethink the shower thing." Evan kissed her cheek and held her even tighter. "So, listen. Let's play a game while we wait," he suggested.

"What kind of game?" Patricia asked cautiously. Knowing Evan, his game probably involved testing their bouncibility by jumping down onto the lower roof of the school.

"We get to ask each other five questions, we can't ask why we're asking, and we have to answer honestly," Evan explained.

"Truth or dare, but without the dare?" Patricia asked.

"Basically."

"Evan, that's not a game—that's a conversation," she chided, tilting her neck back to grin up at him.

He used the tip of one finger to brush her hair off her shoulder. His delicate touch sent a shiver down her arm. "Call it what you want," he said. "It'll be fun."

"All right," Patricia agreed. "But I get to ask first."

"Shoot. I'm ready for anything." Evan leaned back on his elbows, and Patricia turned to face him. The breeze was picking up, so she pulled a hair band out of her pocket and twisted her hair into a ponytail as she thought. This game could actually get very interesting . . . if she could come up with a deeply probing, intriguing question. She glanced at a paint stain on his sleeve.

"Okay. What were you painting before you picked me up today?" she asked.

"It stinks," Evan said, rolling his eyes. He pulled his legs up and sat Indian style. "I think I'm gonna toss it." He started to pull at a white string hanging from the hem of his jeans, pointedly staring down and away from her.

She knew Evan was just being hard on himself—he usually was. "What is it of?" she asked.

"The old schoolhouse," he said.

Patricia pictured the little red Laura-Ingalls-Wilder-type schoolhouse in her mind and knew that Evan had probably produced an incredibly haunting painting of it—whether or not he thought it was good. She made a mental note to find the painting the next time she was at his house.

"My turn," Evan told her. "Let's see . . . what color would you want the sky to be if it could be something other than blue all the time?"

Patricia crinkled her forehead. "What kind of question is that?"

"Just think about it for five seconds," Evan urged. He leaned forward, resting his chin in his hands and focusing his intense green eyes on Patricia's face. "I mean, what if the sky were psychedelic orange or crimson or—"

"Well, then I'd think it was nuclear fallout." Patricia laughed. "And nuclear war is never a good thing."

"You have a point. We'll stick with blue." He picked up her hand and started playing with her fingers. "You go."

Patricia bit her lip and chewed on it for a few moments while she watched Evan play her fingers like a piano. There *was* something she really wanted to know, but she wasn't sure she should ask him. The answer could change the whole course of their relationship. Just thinking about it made Patricia start to breathe faster. Then she decided, what the heck? The game was his idea in the first place. And she wanted to know.

"Who was your first love?" she blurted out.

The blush spread over Evan's tan skin faster than you could say "snagged." He looked as if she had just asked him whether he wore boxers or briefs. Actually, that wasn't a bad question either. . . .

"Uh . . ." Evan dropped her fingers and pushed both hands through the curls at his temples—his classic "help me, God" gesture. "Well, who's *your* first love?" he said finally.

"You are so not ducking this question, Schnure," Patricia told him. She was, however, beginning to doubt whether she wanted to hear his answer. Obviously Patricia wanted him to say that she was his first love. She and Evan had been together for two months, and they'd never said those "three little words" to each other. But maybe that was because Evan didn't feel the same way she did. If he did love her, wouldn't he have just answered her? What was with this little game of dodgeball?

"Well, I—I mean, I've had *crushes*," he stammered. He was pulling violently at his jeans now, and Patricia began to wonder when the leg was going to start unraveling. "You've had crushes, right?"

Patricia tried to smile. The boy was seriously avoiding the issue—all she could do at this point was play along. "Like five hundred," she answered. "Let's see . . . Leonardo DiCaprio, James Van Der Beek, Matt Damon—"

"I'm talking about real people!" Evan interrupted with a roll of the eyes. He found Patricia's Hollywood obsession endlessly mock-worthy. "People who exist in the realm of your reality." They both laughed—Patricia's laughter mostly being out of nervousness. "And don't think I haven't noticed that all of your crushes are blond. But we'll get to that later. First tell me if you've had a crush in real life."

Suddenly Patricia started to squirm. There *was* one guy in her past . . . one *blond* guy. He was so amazingly perfect. But he'd been about as aware of her as he would've been of a tiny pebble stuck in the groove on the bottom of his sneaker. Beyond pointless was that crush. So it couldn't hurt to tell Evan about him, right?

"Well, there was one—" She stopped short. She'd heard a car. It had just pulled up below them. Patricia froze. "Oh my gosh. We're dead!" she whispered.

Evan went rigid, which made every nerve in Patricia's body sizzle. He was supposed to be in charge. He was supposed to be the ever confident, I'm-too-lucky-to-get-caught guy. But his eyes were bulging out of his head as if he'd just tasted her grandmother's atomic chili.

"Wait here," he whispered, making a little stop signal with his hand. The car door shut. Feet crunched on gravel.

"What're you gonna do?" Patricia asked, grabbing for his hand even though he'd started crawling away. Patricia held her breath. Evan was making way too much noise.

"Just wait." He didn't look back. He was already at the edge of the roof.

Then the voice. "Hey! Who's up there?"

A pause. Patricia waited for the heart attack to seize her, envisioning a police cruiser, fingerprint cards, flashing lights, her class picture in the police-report section of the paper—

"C'mon. I know someone's up there. I can hear you panting with fear." A chuckle.

Evan looked back at her, and she could tell they were both thinking the same thing. Obviously a teenager. Evan stuck his head out over the wall. Patricia still couldn't move.

9

"Hey, buddy," the voice said. "Who're you? The watchtower guy?"

"Maybe. Who're you?" Evan asked.

A pause. "Rider Marshall."

Patricia sucked wind. And then she almost blacked out. It couldn't be.

She closed her eyes: blond hair. Sea blue eyes. Perfect legs. Rider on the tennis court. Rider drinking from a water fountain—licking a little drip off his lip. Rider in a tux at the club, looking as if he'd just stepped off the red carpet at the Academy Awards.

By the time Patricia had crawled all the way to the edge, she couldn't remember how she'd made it there. She braced her arms and looked down, and it was him. It was actually him! Only he was taller. And blonder. And hotter.

Rider looked at Patricia, and she thought her heart was going to pound out through her chest . . . and fall on the ground right at his feet.

"Rider?" she squeaked. Ugh! Way to sound ridiculous. She cleared her throat. "You're back," she said in a deeper voice. Patricia might have even sounded sexy. She wasn't sure because her whole body was shaking. She felt Evan's eyes on her.

"Patricia?" Rider said. And her elbows almost collapsed.

He remembered her.

Evan hit the ground first. And he checked Rider out before he turned around and helped Patricia down. He couldn't help it. Patricia was obviously affected by this Princeton poster boy, and Evan had to see why. Unfortunately Rider looked like a preppy hybrid of the three so-called actors whom Patricia had just admitted to worshiping. Not a good sign.

Patricia bent over and dusted off her knees before turning to face the guy. From the anticipation he sensed in the air, Evan half expected them to run into each other's arms. But Patricia just stood there, shoved her hands in her pockets, and kicked a couple of times at the grass with her toe. Evan knew this was her nervous gesture—she always went through those motions when she was on deck to bat at a game.

Then she looked up. "Hi," she said to Rider. She grinned. He grinned. This was trouble.

"Patricia Carpenter." Rider folded his arms across his chest and actually looked her over as if she were there to buy. Evan had to clasp his hands behind his head to keep from doing something stupid—like punching Rider in the face and then cowering on the ground while he got his butt kicked. Rider *was* bigger than him. "How've you been?" Rider asked.

"Fine! Great! I've been great!" Patricia answered—far too enthusiastically. "What're you doing here?"

"My dad got transferred back, so he pulled me out of that stuffy New England prep school . . . thank God," the Golden Boy answered, fiddling

11

with the cuffs of his pristine white shirt. "Actually, I kind of begged him to let me finish out senior year here," he said with a grin. "I'm starting classes on Monday."

"Really?" she squealed. Evan blinked. His girlfriend had squealed. *Very* bad sign. "That's great. Really . . . um . . . great." Okay, and she was also becoming illiterate. Evan decided it was time for him to step in.

"Hey, man," he said, stepping forward and offering his hand. "I'm Evan Schnure."

Rider looked at Evan's hand for a second before clasping it. "Hey. Rider Marshall." Strong grip. It figured.

"Yeah. You said that already," Evan reminded him with an overly polite smile.

Rider laughed. "I guess I did. Well, I'd better go," he told them, rubbing his hands together and looking around. "I just wanted to check the old place out."

"Right. Well . . . yeah. Okay," Patricia said. She giggled, and Evan almost laughed at how silly she sounded. Only it wasn't so funny when he thought about the fact that this guy had reduced his normally rational girlfriend to an incoherent babbler.

"Okay, then. Guess I'll see you on Monday," he said, slipping on a pair of dark sunglasses. He turned and opened the door of his car—a jet-black, vintage Mustang convertible. "Nice meeting you . . . Evan?"

"Yep. You too, Rider," Evan responded, rocking back and forth on his heels.

Rider gunned the engine and peeled out of the parking lot, disappearing behind a line of trees. Evan waited to hear him turn with a screech of tires onto the main drag before he looked at Patricia. She was a zombie.

"So, I take it you *have* had a crush before," Evan said, throwing his arm around her shoulders.

Patricia suddenly snapped to. "Huh?" she asked, blinking up at him with her beautiful blue eyes. "What? Rider? No, he wasn't a crush."

"Was he a *boyfriend?*"

That cracked her up. "No *way.*" She laughed. "He's two years older than us! Plus every single girl at the country club wanted him." She suddenly blushed scarlet.

"So he *was* a crush," Evan stated, starting to walk toward his moped. This outing hadn't gone at all like he'd planned. Instead of having a romantic afternoon, they had missed the glorious sunset for their riveting conversation with Rider. A guy who Patricia had obviously drooled over from afar.

"I guess so," she admitted. "I'm sorry. I was just surprised to see him again. He moved away, like, over two years ago. It was a silly eighth-grade thing. It was the cool thing to do to follow him around like a puppy dog. I can't believe how stupid we all were. He's really not all that." She shrugged and did a good job of looking totally unaffected. But Evan wanted her to actually *be* unaffected.

He slipped one hand under her hair, cupped the back of her neck with his fingers, and pulled her to him. It was what Evan fondly referred to as a "soap-opera kiss." He held her for an extra-long time, enjoying her closeness, her soft skin, and the always astounding feeling that, as she returned the kiss, she really wanted to be there with him.

It took Patricia a couple of seconds to open her eyes after Evan pulled away. When she did, she stared straight into the depths of him. As usual, his heart responded with an elaborate thump.

"What was that for?" she asked.

"For being with me," Evan answered, touching his forehead to hers. "I'm dreading the day you wake up and see me for the troll that I am."

"I don't kiss trolls," she said. She leaned in slightly and pressed her lips to his, wrapping her arms around him tightly.

Ah, yes. This was much better. Evan had a feeling Rider was already forgotten.

At least he could hope that was true.

TWO

"*RIDER MARSHALL?*" COURTNEY screeched, grabbing Patricia's wrist.

"*The* Rider Marshall?" Isabel chimed in, snatching her other hand.

Patricia nodded, looking at her two best friends with a justifiably self-satisfied expression. Then they all screamed—"*Ahhhhh!*"—as if they'd just won a radio contest.

Patricia was beaming, and she couldn't help it. The former object of their obsession was back in town, and *she* had been the first one to see him. This was the kind of felicity that never came her way. Courtney Sanders was Patricia's tall, runway-worthy, rich friend who always got what she wanted. Isabel Vasquez was her athletic, ambitious, risk-taker friend who always worked her butt off . . . and got what she wanted. And Patricia was just Patricia Carpenter—the moderately cute one who

15

occasionally stumbled upon some dumb luck. This was her finest hour.

"Tell us everything," Courtney ordered, pulling Patricia toward one of the lounge chairs by the pool in Patricia's backyard. "Was he still beautiful?"

"What was he wearing?" Isabel added.

"What was he *driving?*" Courtney asked.

Patricia laughed and ran her fingers through her hair, pushing it back behind her shoulders. Her friends were now both sitting across from her, sharing one sunflower-print chair and leaning forward in rapt anticipation. They looked like kids in line at an ice-cream truck. Patricia decided to savor the attention.

"Well . . . he looked . . . *okay,* I guess," she said. "Pretty much the same, really." Patricia saw their faces start to fall. "Except even more perfect!"

"Are you serious?" Courtney asked in awe.

"Is that even possible?" Isabel added.

"Oh, it's not only possible, it's confirmed," Patricia said, twisting her hair up into a knot at the top of her head. She leaned back nonchalantly and stretched her legs out on the chair, letting the afternoon sun warm her skin. She felt like a movie star surrounded by salivating fans, hanging on her every word. "He was taller, and broader, and blonder, and . . . he was driving a vintage Mustang convertible."

"Shut *up!*" Isabel exclaimed, slapping Patricia's leg. The Mustang was Isabel's dream car.

"What's so big about a Mustang?" Courtney

asked, getting up and striding over to the third chair. "It's not like a Boxster or a Hummer or anything." She plopped down, picked up her sunglasses, and pushed them up on top of her head to hold her short black hair off her face.

"I'm not even going to dignify that with a response," Isabel said haughtily, lying back in her own chair.

"Whatever," Courtney said, examining her nails. "I want to hear more about Rider anyway. Patricia, when are you going to dump Evan?"

"What?" Patricia and Isabel said at the same time, whipping their heads around to face Courtney.

Dump Evan? Patricia thought. *Why would I do that?* "What does Evan have to do with anything?" she demanded.

"Isn't it obvious?" Courtney asked, rubbing a blob of suntan lotion into her paler-than-flour skin. "It was fate that you bumped into Rider. You two were meant to be together." She smiled. "I bet you end up a couple before your birthday."

Patricia paused. Her sixteenth birthday was a week away. "You expect me to dump my boyfriend and snag Rider by next Sunday?"

"Exactly," Courtney said.

Patricia looked at Isabel, and they both laughed. "That would be very ambitious of me," Patricia responded. "But I might as well do *something* interesting since no one's throwing me a party or anything." Patricia watched her friends out of the corner of her eye as they tried not to

17

look at each other. She knew they'd been planning a surprise party for her for weeks. She just didn't know which night it was going to take place.

Courtney sat up, turned, and planted her bare feet on the ground, studying Patricia. "Don't try to change the subject. You and Rider go together. Jeez, look at the two of you. You're practically Barbie and Ken."

Patricia laughed. She might have the blond hair and blue eyes, but with her athletic, five-foot, two-inch frame and nowhere-near-*Baywatch* bod, she wasn't quite Barbie. "There are so many things wrong with that analogy, I can't even begin to list them," Isabel said, shaking her head in disbelief.

"Seriously, Court. And if Rider and I were fated to bump into each other so that true love could blossom, what the heck was Evan doing there with me?" Patricia asked, raising her eyebrows.

"Details." Courtney waved her hand as if to swat that little snag away. "Rider always liked you best."

Courtney's declaration made Patricia's whole body tense up with excitement. "What do you mean?" she asked. "He didn't even know any of us was alive."

"I have to go with Courtney on this one, P.," Isabel interjected, tilting her face toward the sun. "He didn't know either of *us* existed, but he was quite aware of *you*. Remember that night at the country club when he asked you to dance—*twice?*"

"Well, yeah . . . ," Patricia began.

"And the rest of us all spent the night in the corner, stuffing our faces with fried calamari and turning green with envy," Courtney prompted.

"Then the next day we were all turning green from the fried calamari!" Isabel added. Both Isabel and Courtney dissolved into laughter. But Patricia's brain was now in hyperdrive.

She remembered those two dances with Rider. She'd played and replayed them over in her mind a thousand times, wondering if she'd looked okay, if she'd said the right things, if she'd had lettuce stuck in her teeth. Patricia knew Rider had picked her out of a crowd, and she knew that everyone was insane with jealousy, but she had talked herself down with logic. She'd simply been nearby when Rider had decided he felt like dancing. He'd never *liked* her. Right?

"I think the sun is affecting your brains," Patricia announced finally. "Those dances were just a well-mannered guy taking pity on a midget geek with braces. Besides, Courtney, just because you think Evan isn't good enough for me or whatever, that doesn't mean I'm going to drop him when the first Ken doll comes along."

"Yeah!" Isabel agreed. "Evan's a sweetie."

"Uh, excuse me, but I didn't think it was so sweet when he organized a protest against football-team funding during the most important game of the year," Courtney scoffed. "And it wasn't *sweet* when he spray-painted Mr. Grassi's classroom door just because he yelled at Evan for drawing a caricature of him."

Patricia chewed her lip. Evan did act sort of immature when he didn't get his way.

"Face it, Patricia," Courtney added. "Evan is a complete jerk to anyone who has opinions he doesn't like. And I don't see what's so great about having a boyfriend who spends half his time in detention and the other half swimming in turpentine."

Patricia sighed. Courtney didn't like Evan, and Evan didn't like her. Whenever the two of them got together, sarcasm slinging ensued. Courtney had latched on to the fact that Evan was less than popular, and Evan had focused on Courtney's preoccupation with appearances. Patricia just wished they could both take off the blinders and see the good parts about each other.

"Court, Evan is my boyfriend and he's going to be around for a long time, so you'd better get used to it." Patricia closed her eyes and leaned back, signaling that the subject was officially dropped.

But it wasn't, really—at least not for her. Isabel and Courtney moved on to discussing the party Mr. Sanders was throwing for Courtney's brother that night. Good old Troy had finally passed the bar exam after about five tries, and the Sanderses would use any excuse to hire caterers. But Patricia found her thoughts returning to Rider. Her palms started to sweat, and it took some painful effort to prevent a huge grin from spreading across her face. First of all, her friends were jealous of her, and that was enough to merit a little smirk. But what if they were right? What if Rider had picked her back then for a reason?

Patricia shivered all over and had to wrap her arms around herself so that her friends wouldn't notice. *Me and Rider.* Imagine. Suddenly Patricia saw herself standing by the rosebushes at the club on a crisp, clear night. Stars dotted the sky as she looked out over the lake. Her flowing white dress fluttered in the breeze, and she turned, sensing someone was there. Watching. Then Rider stepped out of the shadows and into the moonlight. He fixed his deep blue eyes on hers, took her hand in his, and said—

"Hey! Space cadet!" Patricia's eyes popped open, and she blushed beet red. Courtney was standing over her, snapping her fingers.

"I am *not* breaking up with Evan," Patricia blurted out quickly. "I'd have to be insane."

Courtney smirked. "Try to keep up, Patricia. We moved on from that subject fifteen minutes ago." She placed her hands on her hips. "What were you just thinking about anyway? You're all smiley. Could it be Rider?"

Patricia thought fast. She was not about to own up to her traitorous fantasies. "No. I was just . . . uh . . . dozing off, that's all. Maybe I started to dream or something."

"Uh-huh," Courtney said with an "I-am-so-sure" nod. "Well, we're gonna go get ready for the party."

21

"Yeah. We'll see you and Evan there, right?" Isabel asked as she stuffed her things into her mesh bag and stood up.

"Of course! Yeah! Why wouldn't we be there?" Patricia jumped out of her chair, visions of Rider still dancing through her mind. Patricia could practically feel the touch of his fingers on hers. This was not a good thing. *Think about Evan—your boyfriend,* she told herself. "I'll walk you guys out."

She led them through the sliding-glass doors into the kitchen and tiptoed through the house. Patricia's mom was out, and her dad was working in the study. He worked at home all week, so Patricia's friends were programmed for silence between the hours of nine A.M. and five P.M. Normally he wouldn't be working on a Sunday, but he was a writer and had a big deadline to meet.

As they made their way through the living room, Patricia glanced at the study door. Maybe her ever-creative father would have an idea on how to deal with these disloyal Rider thoughts. Right. Both her parents would probably just side with Courtney and tell her to dump Evan. Neither of them was very psyched that their daughter was dating the town screwup. Patricia sighed.

"See you later, guys!" she said as Isabel and Courtney opened the door and skipped down the steps toward Courtney's car. Courtney had an early birthday, so she'd gotten her license before the rest of the class—her dad had bought her a Land Rover. Typical.

"Bye, Patricia. Think about what I said!" Courtney called. Isabel looked back at Patricia and rolled her eyes before getting in the car.

"I saw that!" Courtney said.

Patricia laughed and closed the door, leaning back on the solid oak for support. She was suddenly very tired, and all she could think about was her encounter with Rider. She had sounded like such a moron in front of him—*and* Evan. It was as if her tongue had knotted itself up and refused to move. And she couldn't believe how cool Evan had been about it. He'd totally noticed her jellyfishlike state. He could have been pissed, or jealous, or at least miffed, but he was understanding instead. This was rare in guys her age. She was so lucky to have him.

Suddenly she remembered the feeling of Evan's incredible lips on hers. He made her feel so . . . beautiful . . . perfect . . . wanted. What she needed was some serious quality time with her boy. Then all thoughts of Rider Marshall would fade back to the realm of childhood daydreams, where they belonged.

Evan closed his eyes and imagined he was at the ocean. The waves slapping at the shore, bubbles gurgling around rocks, the muffled horn of some faraway ship . . . his mother taking out the garbage. As the heavy, metal trash can lid clattered into place, he glanced over and saw his mom gazing at him admiringly.

"I love that dreamy look you get on your face

when you're painting," she said. "It reminds me of when you were a baby."

"Ugh! Mom, please," Evan said, throwing a reasonably clean towel in her direction. She caught it, twirled it around, and whipped him on the butt with it. "Ow!"

"Be nice to your dear old mom," she said, pushing a red spiral curl out of her eyes. "I've had a long day. The Burko twins were here for eight hours."

Evan shuddered. "Sorry," he said, looking back at his seascape painting. "I was just trying to feel the ocean."

She came over and stood next to him, examining the painting he was working on for Patricia's birthday. He had decided on an evening ocean scene, taken from her favorite spot on the beach. She was going to flip out when she saw it.

"It's beautiful, Ev," his mom said, ruffling his hair as if he were a five-year-old. He couldn't blame her, though. She ran a baby-sitting business out of the house and spent most of her day with people two feet tall and under. She'd been in business for herself ever since Evan's dad left when Evan was two. "I don't know where you got this talent from, but let's just say it was from my side of the family and it skipped my generation."

"It's all you, Mom."

She grinned. "You asked me to remind you when party time got close. Patricia's mom will be dropping her off any minute," she said.

"Right," Evan said, glancing at the old alarm clock on top of the laundry machine. "Thanks."

She went back inside, closing the garage door behind her. Evan had turned the two-car garage into a makeshift studio back in middle school. His mom always parked her tan minivan in the driveway, so aside from the garbage cans, lawn mower, and washer and dryer, he had the whole space to himself. He looked around, thinking not for the first time of how lucky he was. Paintings in various stages of completion leaned against the garage doors. Shelves of paints, pencils, pads, canvases, rags, turpentine, brushes, sponges, and all sorts of tools lined the back wall. The only thing better than the time he spent out here alone was the time when Patricia was here with him.

Evan took a deep breath and smiled, remembering when Patricia first walked into his life. He had always sort of known her. She was a pretty athlete, a decent student, and popular in a quiet kind of way. He'd been completely shocked when she and her friend Isabel stepped into his choir rehearsal at the beginning of the year. Most of the choir members were surprised—it was a fairly closed crowd. But the moment Patricia opened her mouth to sing, Evan was blown away. She had the most incredible voice, and she sang with so much emotion. And before he knew it, the two of them were talking more than they were singing.

"Evan? Are you in there?" Evan jumped at the sound of her voice. Patricia was right outside. He could see the top of her ponytail through one of the grimy garage-door windows.

"Just a sec!" Evan called as he fumbled with her painting. He had to hide it somewhere. He picked it up with both hands flat against the sides so he wouldn't touch the wet parts. He looked left. He looked right. There was no place for it. He finally put the painting down again and grabbed an easel, standing it near the corner. The easel fell over with a clatter.

"What? Do you have another girl in there?" she asked.

Evan laughed nervously and picked up the easel again. "Yes! Can you at least give her some time to get out the back window?" With shaking hands he finally got the easel to stay and faced it toward the back wall. Then he grabbed the painting and placed it carefully on top.

"Nope! I'm comin' in!" she shouted.

Evan bounded across the room and stuck his hands under the faucet of the big metal sink. Patricia opened the side door just as he was turning on the water. She looked around, and her face creased with fake disappointment.

"I missed her?" she asked.

"Sorry. She's pretty fast," he answered, drying his hands.

"I'll bet," she joked. She walked over to the empty easel where her painting had been. "What were you working on?" she asked.

Evan glanced around. Good question. His eyes fell on his project for the arts festival at school. "I was just finishing up my entry," he said, nodding in the direction of the painting.

Patricia walked across the cold concrete floor and picked it up. Then she placed it on the easel and stepped back. "Evan, it's so incredible," she said. "The woman looks so dark and . . . lonely."

"Really? You think so?" Evan asked, climbing over a rolled-up rug to stand next to her. "That's exactly what I was going for."

"Well, you did it," Patricia told him. Evan looked at her profile, watching her as she pressed her lips together in concentration. They were tinted pink with gloss, and her skin looked perfect, her blond hair swept away from her face. Evan realized, not for the first time, how incredibly lucky he was to have this beautiful, talented, intuitive girl in his presence, let alone as his girlfriend. It was unbelievable.

He put his arms around her from behind, rested his chin on her shoulder and studied the painting with her. As she nestled against him, his heart started to pound and he had the urge to tell her he loved her. But the thought made his mouth go dry and his tongue swell. He couldn't do it. What if she didn't say it back? Or worse, what if she laughed at him?

Then again, why had she asked him that question last night? She wanted him to tell her he loved her, right? Why would she have brought it up if she didn't? He couldn't think of a reason.

Yeah, right, Evan thought suddenly, his insecurities kicking in. *Who am I kidding?* Patricia Carpenter in love with him? Sure, she was dating him, but get real. There was no way a girl as perfect as her could love a screwup like him.

"You know, if you want to stay here and keep working, I'll totally understand," Patricia said, breaking into his thoughts and forcing him to compose himself. "I know how much this festival means to you."

"Can't get rid of me that easily," Evan said. He kissed her cheek quickly. "Just give me five minutes to clean up inside."

"I'll wait outside," Patricia said.

"Okay." Evan paused at the door to the house and looked back at her as she headed out. This was stupid. He could tell her. He had to tell her. He opened his mouth and almost called her back. But he hesitated, and she disappeared out the door.

Evan shook his head. "Wimp."

"They call this a barbecue?" Evan asked in obvious disbelief as his eyes roamed around the Sanderses' sprawling backyard. Tables covered by white cloths dotted the huge brick patio, candles floated on the surface of the Olympic-size swimming pool, and a wait staff of about thirty people rushed around. There was even a classical quartet set up near the pool house. Patricia spotted a guy in a French chef's hat, fiddling with crabmeat on an open grill.

"Well, they do have charcoal," she offered.

"Patricia! I'm so glad you could come!" Courtney suddenly appeared and grabbed Patricia up in a hug. When she let go, she flicked her gaze in Evan's direction. "Hi, Evan," she said.

"Hi," Evan answered just as coolly.

Courtney stopped a passing waiter. "Could we have some hors d'oeuvres over here?" The waiter bowed slightly, holding the shiny, doily-covered

28

tray in front of them. Patricia surveyed the choices. Caviar, crab cakes, fried calamari, and some unidentifiable green blobby things.

"Um . . . no thanks," Patricia said quickly.

"We're saving ourselves for the main course," Evan put in.

Courtney smiled at Patricia. "Sooner or later you're going to have to graduate from PB and J," she said with a laugh. "I'll catch you later. I have to go talk to my aunt Gena. If you stay away from her for more than five minutes, she forgets who you are."

"Have fun," Patricia said wryly.

As soon as her friend was gone, Patricia and Evan glanced at each other and smiled.

"Kids' table?" he suggested.

"Kids' table," she agreed. Evan grabbed Patricia's hand and they took off, laughing, for the far side of the yard. Next to the custom-made swing set that Mr. Sanders had commissioned for Courtney's twin half sisters was a huge buffet for tiny tots. Hot dogs, burgers, grilled chicken, mac and cheese, fries, beans, and potato salad were set out on a picnic table. Every condiment, soda, and flavor of Hawaiian Punch that Patricia could have imagined was represented, plus a platter full of peanut-butter-and-jelly sandwiches. It was like heaven.

She grabbed some paper plates, handed one to Evan, and joined the line. Evan loaded up enough food to feed a small country, and Patricia took small portions of almost everything.

"Let's go to the gazebo," Patricia suggested as Evan poured her a soda.

"Your wish is my command," Evan said.

Patricia laughed. "Do you think you could lay it on a little thicker?"

Evan shrugged. "I do what I can."

She led him toward the gazebo down by the pond. On the way Patricia saw Isabel with their friend Max Regan and waved. She felt a little guilty for passing them by, but Patricia was psyched to get Evan alone. She felt bad about Rider interrupting their romantic sunset the night before, and she wanted to make up for lost time.

Evan settled onto the bench that lined the inside of the large gazebo. He looked out over the pond, and Patricia watched his face as he took it all in. Whenever he was presented with a new landscape, he studied it as if it were already a work of art.

"This is nice," he said after a moment. "Do you think Courtney's dad would let me paint back here?"

"Not if Courtney had anything to say about it," Patricia told him, taking a bite of her hot dog.

"Ugh! She's so annoying," Evan said in between mouthfuls.

"Can we please not talk about my best friend that way?" Patricia asked. "Let's just have a good time, all right?"

Evan's face softened. "I'm sorry, Patricia. I'll try not to rag on her so much."

"Thanks." He looked depressed now, probably from guilt, which she didn't want. Courtney was just as much to blame for their bickering as Evan. In fact, she was usually the instigator. "You know what we should do? We should finish that game we started last night," she suggested.

Evan brightened up, taking a swig of his Sprite. Then he slapped his hands together and turned toward her, all anticipation. "Right. Your turn," he said.

Patricia thought about it for a second and realized that she had actually been the one to ask the last question . . . the love question, which he'd so deftly avoided. She didn't feel like getting into that territory again, so she decided to just humor him. In fact, she knew exactly what to ask him this time.

Patricia smiled and sat up straight as Evan brought his soda cup to his lips. "Okay, what did you get me for my birthday?"

Evan's flimsy plastic cup slipped from his hands, hitting the bench between them. Patricia's legs were suddenly splattered with cold wetness. One drop flew up and pegged her on the nose.

She and Evan both jumped up. "Oh, man, Patricia, I am so sorry. Is it bad? Are you okay?"

"I'm not wounded, Evan. I'm fine," Patricia said. She just had Sprite splatters all over the skirt of her dress. She watched Evan as he checked under their plates for something and then scrounged in the pockets of his khakis. "What're you doing?" she asked. Her legs felt sticky, so she wiped them and found the Sprite was drying on her skin. Lovely.

"Napkins," he said. "We need napkins. I'll be

right back." He kissed Patricia on the cheek, apologized again, and took off.

"Evan! You really don't have to—" But he was already halfway across the lawn, dodging guests. Patricia stood and then sat back down a few feet away from their plates, where the projectile Sprite hadn't landed. She brushed her skirt a couple of times with no effect, then realized that Evan had once again narrowly avoided answering her question. What was up with that?

Not that she'd really expected him to tell her about her gift, but he was the one who'd invented the rules of the silly game, and now he was breaking them. Had he dropped his soda on purpose to avoid answering? Maybe he'd forgotten about her birthday and hadn't bothered to get her anything yet. Nah. Evan was far too romantic for that.

She sighed and looked out at the water, telling herself to think about something else. A couple of swans were circling in the center of the pond, making perfectly circular ripples. Patricia wondered if Mr. Sanders had paid the birds in seed so that they would swim that way. The thought made her giggle, and she put her hand over her mouth, even though there was no one around to hear.

"What's so funny?" a voice asked.

Patricia's heart skipped a beat.

She stood up—Rider was standing at the foot of the gazebo stairs. At that moment the quartet started playing Vivaldi's *Four Seasons*. Her breath caught in her throat, and she pushed some stray hairs behind her ears. It was just like her daydream! Only it was dusk and not night, and the pond was much smaller than the lake at the club, and she was standing next to half-eaten food instead of roses, and her dress was covered with Sprite.

Patricia sat down, crossed her legs, and turned her soda-soaked side away from Rider. "Rider! Hi!" She fiddled with her skirt. *Stop fidgeting!* she told herself. *Stop it!*

"Hi." He climbed the steps, crossed the gazebo, and sat beside her. His knee grazed Patricia's, and her insides turned to goo. She had to get a grip—now.

"So, here we are again," he said, gracing her with a perfect smile. He was wearing a blue linen shirt that made his eyes look like sapphires.

"Yeah. We have to stop meeting like this," Patricia said. Okay, so she was drowning in her lameness. But at least she had completed a sentence. That was progress. And he was still smiling.

"Oh, hey," he said suddenly. "You have something on your cheek."

Patricia was instantly mortified. Her hands flew to her face, but Rider leaned over and gently touched her cheekbone up near her ear. He delicately wiped whatever it was—probably Sprite—from her skin. And maybe she imagined this, but she could've sworn he let his hand linger there for a moment longer than necessary. Their eyes locked. Patricia felt the air between them sizzle.

If only Courtney and Isabel could have seen *this*.

THREE

IT'S OBVIOUSLY TIME for me to seek help, Evan thought, rolling up a pile of napkins and stuffing them in his pocket. If he was going to keep Patricia interested, he was going to have to refrain from certain things . . . like being a klutz and ruining her dresses. This was not the way to gain points. At least he'd avoided coming up with a good question ducker. The rules of the game specifically stated that honest answers were required, but he wasn't about to tell Patricia about her birthday surprise. Still, she'd probably want an answer when he returned. Maybe he could plead the Fifth.

Evan was so busy mulling this over, he didn't notice Courtney until he was close enough to smell her overpowering perfume.

"Hello, Evan." She'd mastered the art of making a greeting sound condescending.

"Courtney, I'm sure you have a highly creative

insult to throw my way, but unfortunately I just don't have time right now." Evan kept walking. Courtney stepped in front of him. He stopped and rolled his eyes into the back of his head. *Why me?*

"You're right. You are out of time," she said, narrowing her eyes at him.

"Meaning . . . ?"

"Meaning, I think you've already left Patricia alone for too long," she said, smiling brightly. "Things happen, you know."

"Okay, I give," Evan said, looking over Courtney's shoulder toward the gazebo. She, quite helpfully, stepped out of his way so that he could have a full view—a full view of Patricia sitting so close to Rider that their blond heads were practically touching.

Evan felt his hastily scarfed burger shift in his stomach but forced his face into an expression of total calm. "Nothing's happening, Courtney," he said confidently. "Patricia's just catching up with the guy."

"Good act, Evan. But there's no way Rider doesn't intimidate you. You're shakin' in your Skechers right now. Admit it."

She was having far too much fun with this. Evan opened his mouth for a verbal slam, but Isabel stepped in out of nowhere.

"What's Rider doing here?" she asked.

That was exactly what Evan wanted to know. He looked over at the gazebo, where Patricia and Rider were both laughing. Evan had a flash fantasy of putting Rider in a choke hold.

"When my dad found out the Marshalls were

back in town, he invited them right away," Courtney explained with a self-satisfied smile. "Doesn't he look amazing?"

"He did get better looking," Isabel agreed.

Great. And Evan had always trusted her to be the normal one—the one on his side.

"Yeah. *Patricia* was right about that," Courtney said, shooting Evan a glance to make sure he'd caught what she said. He had. It was about as subtle as a baseball bat to the head.

"Court*ney,*" Isabel scolded.

"What?" Courtney asked, all innocence. "He *is* better looking. I would go after him myself if he didn't so obviously want Patricia. He's a lost cause."

"Courtney!" Isabel grabbed her wrist. But it didn't matter. The damage was done. Evan had had enough of this conversation.

Without even a blink at either of the girls, Evan marched across the yard toward the gazebo, his eyes focused on Rider. He wanted to walk right up to the guy and tackle him into the pond. Of course, that probably wouldn't go over well with Mr. Sanders. Maybe Evan would just tell Rider off. But if Rider started pushing Evan around, Evan would be the one to get kicked out anyway. He was the black sheep at these country-club-type functions. It seemed like everyone from the groundskeeper to the guest of honor knew he was the town rebel. The kid who was in perpetual detention all through middle school for such major offenses as fighting with a teacher who called Evan's friend an idiot and cutting out of school to go to the lecture of a well-known artist in town. A real criminal mastermind.

Evan stomped up the steps, making sure he was loud enough to get Patricia and Rider's attention. Patricia stood and wiped her hands on the back of her dress. Evan didn't miss the significance of that gesture. Sweaty palms meant crush. He had to get Patricia away from this guy as soon as possible.

"Evan, you remember Rider, right?" she said quickly.

"Yeah, hey, man," Evan said, barely glancing at Rider. He was focused on his slightly flushed girlfriend.

"Hey," Rider answered.

"Listen, Patricia, do you mind if we bail?" *Please say fine. Please say fine. Please say fine,* Evan pleaded silently.

"Why?"

Great. "I just realized how much work I have to finish before tomorrow, and it's getting kind of late," Evan said, glancing at his wrist—as if he ever wore a watch.

"Oh. The painting?" Her delicate eyebrows scrunched up in concern.

"Yeah. I want to make sure it's ready for tomorrow," Evan said. He was such a dork. The painting was ready. It had been ready for days, and he'd promised himself he wouldn't touch it again. He just couldn't handle the idea of his girlfriend hanging with Rider the Magnificent Senior Stud for a moment longer.

"He's entering a painting in the arts festival," Patricia said to Rider.

"It's kind of important," Evan added, wondering why he was explaining himself to this guy.

"Oh. Well. That's cool," Rider commented.

Cool. Right. He probably didn't know art from ESPN. "So, can we go?" Evan asked Patricia.

"Sure," she said with a smile. "I have some homework to finish up anyway. I've been slacking."

Relief washed over Evan like a cool breeze. Patricia walked over to him and took his hand. "Bye, Rider," she said.

"Catch you later," he answered, lifting his chin.

As they started to walk, Evan handed Patricia the napkins and let out a deep breath. Patricia hadn't chosen to stay with Rider. She was leaving with him. Evan felt like he was on top of the world.

"I have to go say good-bye to Courtney," Patricia said suddenly. "I'll be right back." She jogged over to where Courtney and Isabel were standing. Evan watched Courtney, who was obviously urging Patricia to stay at the party and let him go without her. He could just imagine her arguments. "I'll drive you home. You don't want to sit on the back of his *moped* anyway, do you?"

Finally Patricia turned around and walked back toward Evan, smiling. Courtney shot him an irritated look, and he grinned back smugly. He couldn't help it.

Round one is mine.

Patricia closed her eyes, wrapped her arms more tightly around Evan's waist, and rested her cheek against his back.

"Don't fall asleep back there," Evan joked as he maneuvered his bike around a turn.

"Don't worry about me," Patricia told him. "I'm just getting comfy." The breeze whipped her dress against her thighs, and she smiled contentedly. She loved riding on Evan's moped—especially on unusually warm evenings like this one. She would pretend it was a big Harley-Davidson and they were both clad in worn jeans and leather jackets, heading across the country to California. It made her feel as if they could do anything and no one mattered but the two of them.

Evan lurched to a stop in front of Patricia's house, and she reluctantly climbed off the moped. She pulled off her helmet and fastened it to the back of the bike. Evan took his off too, and a bunch of his curls stuck straight up.

"So, are you okay?" Patricia asked, running her fingers through his messy mop. "Back at Courtney's you looked like you were going to throw up."

He blushed a little. "No. I'm fine," he said. "I'm sorry for making you leave. I could always run you back and your mom could pick you up later."

Patricia contemplated the idea for a moment. She imagined herself walking through the yard in a new, nonsplattered dress and finding Rider by the pond, waiting for her. Then she mentally smacked herself. Her boyfriend was sitting in front of her and she was thinking about Rider! She looked down the road from where they'd come and shrugged. "Nah. That's okay. I wasn't kidding about my homework. There is a ton of French verbs calling my name."

Evan laughed. "Don't spend too much time with them," he said. "I'm beginning to get jealous of your French book."

"Don't be." Patricia grinned. "It has none of your personality, believe me." She leaned over and kissed him on the lips. He reached up and touched her cheek with his hand. Patricia loved how he always wanted to touch her—as if he was appreciating every moment with her.

"Good luck with the painting," Patricia said, pulling away.

He blinked, looking confused. "Thanks. Well, I guess I should go." He refastened his helmet and gave her a half smile. "I'll call you later."

"You'd better." Patricia stepped away so that he could go. He waved as he drove off.

She watched until he was a few blocks off and then turned around to face her house. Patricia didn't really feel like dealing with *le français* right now. It was too nice a night to waste on conjugation. Maybe she *could* go back to the party . . . to Rider. Her mom would drive her.

Patricia laughed, walking up the path toward her porch. Like Rider would really be waiting for her. Sure, they'd had a nice conversation about school and the tennis team and everything, but it wasn't like he was interested in her. Especially since she'd made that stupid comment about his cool socks and had spit on herself once while talking. She was sure he was completely disenchanted and just being polite.

But he had looked just like a movie star. And he

had sat alone with her for a while when there were tons of other people he could have talked to. Maybe he *was* disappointed that she'd left. Maybe if she went back . . . imagine. Just imagine having a senior boyfriend. A guy she'd wanted since the beginning of time—

What was she thinking? Patricia dropped onto the porch swing, consumed with guilt. Why did Rider still have that effect on her after all this time? Patricia had Evan now, but she was still thinking about Rider as a potential boyfriend.

But she *wanted* to be with Evan. He was the most incredible guy she'd ever known—adventurous and artistic and thoughtful and sensitive. And she didn't want to lose him. In fact, she was pretty sure she was in love with him—even if it seemed the *L* word was the last thing on his mind.

She pushed her foot against the aging plank floor of the porch and sent the swing creaking back and forth. This was it. She was going to stop letting herself get sucked back into her eighth-grade fantasies. She was going to avoid making an idiot of herself in front of Rider, who undoubtedly wasn't even interested in a not yet totally filled out sophomore like herself. She was going to wise up before she embarrassed herself and did something stupid that would make Evan hate her forever.

Patricia leaned her elbow on the arm of the swing and sighed.

She was going to stay away from Rider Marshall. She could do that . . . for love.

FOUR

"RIDER? OH MY gosh! It *is* you! How *are* you?"

Evan gripped the painting under his arm and resisted the urge to stick his finger down his throat. He'd been walking behind Rider in the hall for all of thirty seconds and already ten people had practically fallen at his feet. Five girls, two guys, two teachers, and a janitor. You'd think JFK had come back from the dead. All this for a guy who swung his butt while he walked.

"Welcome back, Rider." Evan smirked as he watched Rider stop in front of Ms. DeCaro. This was where the worship would stop. The gym teacher would never fall for his act.

"Thanks, Ms. DeCaro," Rider said, grinning. "I really missed Jamesport High while I was away. But I probably missed your workouts in gym class the most."

She blushed. *Oh, come on!* Evan couldn't believe what he was seeing.

"We'll whip you right back into shape, Mr. Marshall."

Who *was* this guy anyway? James Bond? Evan pushed through the packed hallway and turned down the art wing.

And there was Patricia. She was standing right next to Mrs. Russo's room, already dressed in her softball uniform. He'd almost forgotten that Monday was game day. Man, what would he do without her? Not only did she remember how important this day was to him, she'd rushed to get ready for her game so that she could be here for him.

Evan forgot all about Rider as the importance of the moment swept over him. He was about to submit his painting for the arts festival. Each year all the works in the festival were judged by a panel from the University of Florida and the top three were sent to a state scholarship competition. But it wasn't just about the money. Evan had put gallons of sweat and tears into this painting, and it was time to lay his soul on the line.

"Hey, you!" Patricia said with a supportive smile. "Are you ready?"

"Piece of cake," Evan told her as confidently as possible.

Obviously Patricia saw right through his cool facade. "It'll be fine," she said, taking his hand. It was like stepping under a waterfall. She had such a calming effect on him. If only he could put into words how much she meant to him.

You could put it into words, he told himself. *Just get your tongue working.* But all he could say was, "Thanks."

"Anytime," she answered. They walked into Mrs. Russo's room together. The sour smell of fresh clay mixed with the scent of drying paint filled the room. Ah. His home away from home.

Mrs. Russo emerged from her office at the far end of the room, all smiles and ruddy excitement. Her blue smock was covered with paint and coffee stains. She was constantly dousing herself with coffee when she got excited—which seemed to happen a lot.

"I thought I heard someone come in!" she said in her patented deep-but-fast manner—like a sexy soap-opera star on caffeine. The voice didn't gel with the short, chubby teacher. "Finally ready for the unveiling, are we?"

Evan grinned as he started to feel his confidence rise. This was his home turf. And Mrs. Russo loved him. She'd never not liked anything he'd done. Evan gave Patricia's hand a squeeze and started to unwrap the painting from its protective brown paper.

"You're gonna love it," Patricia told Mrs. Russo.

"I'm all anticipation," the art teacher answered.

Evan looked at the painting for a moment and sighed. It was the best he'd ever done, hands down. He flipped it around, placed it on the nearest easel, and stepped back to wait for the reaction. His hands immediately went for his hair.

Mrs. Russo's eyebrows shot up, and she started

to smile. Evan caught Patricia's eye, and they both grinned excitedly. But then Patricia's face fell. Evan looked back at Mrs. Russo—she had one hand over her mouth. Her pudgy cheeks were flushed and blotchy, and she was staring at his painting in . . . shock?

"What? What's wrong?" Evan asked. "Does it stink?"

"It's a nude!" she exclaimed, turning her wide eyes on him. She looked as if she half hoped he could deny it.

"Yeah . . ."

"So?" Patricia interjected.

"Well, dear." Mrs. Russo turned and looked at Patricia for some reason—maybe because she couldn't look Evan in the eye. "We can't have nudes in the show. We just can't."

Evan felt the floor drop out from underneath him. It was like stepping off the high dive for the very first time—that elongated moment when the realization hit that the solid world had been left behind. Patricia's distraught face swam before him as he struggled to find his voice in his incredibly dry mouth.

"You just can't, *why?*" he managed finally.

"It's against policy, honey."

"Policy? What policy?" Patricia sounded enraged. *Anger, good,* Evan thought. *Go with that.*

"Yeah! No one told me about this!" he added, stepping next to Patricia and staring the poor woman down. "I've never seen any rules about submissions."

Mrs. Russo started to back away from them as if

they were a pack of advancing wolves. Evan almost felt bad for her, but he was too upset. This couldn't be happening to him.

"Well, I've never *had* to tell anyone before," she said, slumping down into a chair. "It's not about this festival specifically. But the board of education does have guidelines about indecency. They would never allow it."

"Well, what does the board know about art?" Evan demanded. "This isn't indecent! Haven't they ever seen da Vinci? What is this—the Dark Ages?"

"In the Dark Ages you could paint nudes," Patricia pointed out, crossing her arms over her chest.

"Yeah!" he added lamely.

Mrs. Russo's eyes desperately traveled back and forth between Evan and Patricia as if she was looking for the more rational one. She settled on Evan. "I'm sorry, but isn't there something else you could submit?"

Of course there was. Evan had tons of work he could have submitted, but he had chosen this one for a reason. He'd put everything into this painting. And when he was done with it, he was exhausted, but it was a good kind of exhaustion. A satisfying exhaustion. How could he forget about that? How could he relegate this painting that meant so much to him to the wall of his garage?

"I want to submit this one." Okay, that sounded like a whine. Maybe not the best tactic. He lowered his voice and tried again. "Mrs. Russo, I worked very hard on this," he said, staring deep into her eyes and willing her to understand. She was an artist, after all. There had to be something deeper there—a profound understanding between souls whose life pursuit was self-expression.

"I don't doubt it, Evan. It's beautiful."

He was ready to scream. "Then let me show it!" Evan's frustration had him near tears, and he looked to Patricia for support. She took one look at his face and jumped into the ring.

"Look at it, Mrs. Russo," she said, pulling the woman out of her chair by the wrist and positioning her in front of the painting. "Look. It's not necessarily a nude. The lines are all fuzzy, and the girl is blue. She could be, like, blue Flubber or something."

Evan shot her a look.

"What? I'm trying," she said.

"Patricia, I appreciate what you're trying to do," Mrs. Russo said quietly.

She turned to Evan with a sad smile on her face. He swallowed back his emotions and forced himself to go numb before she said: "I just can't accept it."

Patricia felt as if somebody had ripped out her heart. Evan was obviously devastated, but Patricia couldn't believe how strongly she was feeling too. Now he was pacing the floor and avoiding her eyes, which just made her long to hug and comfort him. But the way he'd crossed his arms tightly over his chest kept Patricia from touching him. He looked as if he was about to blow.

"Evan? Are you okay?" she asked quietly.

"Yeah, whatever," he muttered. He ran his hands through his hair. "This stinks so bad. I can't believe the bunch of champion idiots they have running this place."

They both looked over at the door to Mrs. Russo's room. Patricia was waiting for her to come out and offer some words of wisdom or a way to solve things. Wasn't that what teachers were supposed to do? But the door remained closed. "Do you want me to go back in there and get your painting?" she offered.

He stopped pacing and glanced at her, then refocused on the floor. "Nah. Let her have it. Maybe it'll remind her of what a sellout she is!" He shouted the last few words, and Patricia jumped. They were obviously intended for Mrs. Russo to hear.

"Evan," Patricia said through her teeth. He looked at her with what could only be described as surprise—as if he'd forgotten she was there. She gave him a pleading look to calm down. There was a torturous moment of silence, then he turned on his heel and rushed into the deserted front hall.

"Evan! Wait up!" Patricia called, hurrying after him. He stopped abruptly, so she stopped as well, and her cleats squeaked on the linoleum floor.

Her cleats. Her uniform. Her game. Oh, no. Patricia glanced at the hall clock and winced. She had five minutes to make it to the field. And today she was the starting pitcher, so she had to be focused

48

and calm—neither of which she felt right now. If this little meeting had gone how it was supposed to, she and Evan would be walking out there right now, hand in hand, without a care in the world. Maybe it could still be salvaged. Maybe a change of subject would lighten the mood.

Patricia took his hand. He stared at her fingers and rubbed his thumb along the heel of her hand. It was a start. "Why don't you come out to my game?" she said. "Get your mind off this for a little while."

Evan smirked, immediately making her feel that the suggestion was ridiculous. "Thanks, Patricia, but I really need to figure out what I'm gonna do next."

"Do next? What do you mean?"

"I'm not really sure. That's the point," he said. "I just have to do *something*."

Patricia was stung. Evan never missed her games. And this was her first start. He knew how important that was to her. But getting into an argument right now wouldn't help anybody. Besides, Patricia wouldn't be pitching a single ball if she didn't get to the mound.

"Okay, well, I guess I'd better go," she said, hoping he would hear the disappointment in her voice and cave.

Evan reached over and cupped her cheek with his hand. He tried to stare into her eyes, but she looked away. "I promise I'll try to get there before the end of the game."

"Okay," Patricia said, forcing a smile. She felt bad for him. She felt bad for herself. But mostly she just wished Mrs. Russo hadn't slashed a perfectly good afternoon to pieces.

"I'll see you later." He kissed her quickly on the mouth.

"Right. See you," she said. She turned around and started jogging toward the back of the school.

"Good luck, Patricia!" he yelled after her.

"Thanks!" she yelled back, her voice cracking. She actually wanted to cry. The insane emotions of the past few minutes had her all watery and choked up. But she couldn't give in to the urge right now. She had a game to think about. Besides, maybe Evan would get home and just pick another painting for the arts festival. Then he would come to her game and cheer her on as usual.

Patricia rounded a corner and took off at a run. Yeah, he'd be there by the end of the first inning. She knew him. He wouldn't let her down.

Patricia looked left. She looked right. She checked the bases. She checked . . . the stands.

He still wasn't there. Courtney was. So was Rider. And so was her biggest fan—dear old Dad. But all Patricia saw was this big, open void where Evan should have been. She pounded the ball into her glove and swallowed hard. Evan's failure to show didn't change the fact that she had to strike this girl out. The batter was about twice Patricia's size and had a sneer that could send Dirty Harry

50

reeling. The other team hadn't scored on her yet. She was one pitch away from a shutout, but the bases were loaded and her arm felt about as useful as a cold side of beef.

"Go, Buccaneers!" a fan yelled. "This is it!"

Patricia closed her eyes and pushed the doubts away. "I can do this," she whispered.

"Come on, Patricia!" Rider yelled.

He'd been her loudest supporter all day. Patricia held back a smile. No need to break her menacing game face now. One lapse in concentration and she would lose all credibility as a force to be reckoned with.

She wound up and lobbed the ball.

She watched the batter's eyes focus on the ball; saw it spinning toward the plate in slow motion; was mesmerized by a bead of sweat that traveled down the batter's cheek as she pulled back to swing.

She's got it, Patricia realized miserably. *Home run.* All that remained was to wait for the crack of the bat.

The batter missed the ball completely.

Patricia blinked. *I did it,* she thought, stunned. There was a gratifying moment of silence as she stared at the ball in the catcher's glove—and then half the team gang-tackled her to the ground.

"A shutout!" Isabel's voice yelled from the pile. "You pitched a shutout!"

Patricia struggled to her feet, and everyone started jumping up and down. Fans poured out of the stands, and Courtney was by Patricia's side within seconds. She threw her arms around Patricia despite the fact that she was covered in rust-colored dust. That was a big sacrifice for her. Patricia hugged her friend back, grinning like crazy. She couldn't believe it. This was un-doubtedly the most triumphant moment of her entire life.

She opened her eyes and saw her dad striding toward her. She let go of Courtney and ran over to him.

"Daddy!" she yelled, jumping into his arms. She didn't even care who heard her. He hugged her and spun her around. When he set her back down, his ecstatic look mirrored hers.

"Do you realize this is the first shutout in the history of Jamesport softball?" He beamed. "I asked your coach during the sixth inning."

"No! Seriously?" Patricia clutched his forearms as pure elation engulfed her. She'd made history! This would be in the yearbook! It might be in the papers! She could even make Athlete of the Week! Everyone would be talking about Patricia Carpenter's shutout tomorrow.

Well, everyone except Evan. He wouldn't even know about it.

"Hey! Not bad, Patricia!"

She whirled around to find Rider grinning down at her. Immediately she felt shy. She looked at the ground and shrugged, fighting off a blush that would have pushed her over the edge from boiled lobster to four-alarm fire. She didn't need to add to her already blotchy, sweaty unattractiveness. "Yeah, well, I try," she said.

"Are you kidding? You keep that up and we'll have to start selling tickets!"

"Hi, Rider," her dad said, offering his hand. "Nice to see you again."

"You too, sir," Rider answered, shaking her father's hand.

Patricia was smiling so hard, her cheeks hurt.

"Hey, you guys!" Isabel ran over with Max. "A bunch of us are going to The Ridge to celebrate, and the guest of honor has to be there!"

Patricia felt like doing cartwheels. She was the guest of honor. "Think you can handle dinner without me, Dad?"

He gave her his patented proud-papa look. "We always do on game day."

"Thanks!" Patricia kissed him on the cheek and smiled at her friends.

"May I?" Rider asked, offering his arm grandly, as if he were a prince and she were his princess.

Patricia took one last glance around—just to make sure Evan wasn't there. No luck. Where was he anyway? He must have really been upset not to show up at all. *Maybe I should call him,* she thought. *Maybe I should find out how he's doing.*

"Patricia?"

She looked into Rider's blue eyes. He was there for her. He was happy for her. She had been there for Evan earlier that afternoon, but he

wasn't here for her now. And here was this guy—
this gorgeous, coveted, incredibly available guy,
and he was *waiting* for *her.*

Patricia wrapped her arm around Rider's, pulled
the band from her ponytail so that her hair would
cover the sweaty strands stuck to her neck, and took
a deep breath.

"Let's do it," she said.

FIVE

"IF YOU FEEL that strongly about it, you should go to the board of education meeting tomorrow and tell them," Evan's mom said firmly.

Evan and his mother had taken a break from their evening ritual of washing dishes and tidying up to go over his options. Evan had gone back to Mrs. Russo's room and grabbed his painting. Then he'd come home, made some calls, and found out that the illustrious board met on Tuesday evenings at the school and always opened the floor to the community toward the end of the proceedings.

His mother was right. Presenting his case to them was the logical and responsible thing to do.

Of course, what he *wanted* to do was set off the sprinkler system and douse every one of those pretentious—

"What're you thinking, honey?" she asked, laying her hand lightly on his arm.

"Okay, I'll go," Evan said. He picked up a broken orange crayon from the table and peeled back the paper wrapper. Then he grabbed a piece of construction paper and started to draw a caricature of Mrs. Russo.

"Good." She stood up and returned to the sink. "You should get Patricia and some of your other friends to come with you. If you show you have some support, they'll be more likely to go for it."

Not a bad idea. Evan drew a big circle around Mrs. Russo and her pudgy cheeks. He could call his friend Lucas, and Luke would call all the kids from choir. And Evan knew the kids in his art class would be there in a heartbeat. Isabel and Max would definitely show, and maybe Courtney would even come . . . because all the cool kids would be there. Evan sketched in an *X* over Russo's face and colored it in boldly. And maybe Patricia could gather up some of the softball team. There was power in numbers, right?

The softball team. Evan's heart stopped as he looked at the clock over the kitchen sink. It was six o'clock. Patricia's game must have ended long ago, and he hadn't even thought about it since he'd told her he'd try to be there. Evan smacked his forehead with the heel of his hand. What a maggot.

"Mom, I gotta go out for a little while, okay?" he said, pushing back his chair. He had to get to The Ridge. That was the diner where everyone always went after games and concerts and dances and just about everything. Jamesport wasn't much of a town. In grade school everyone rode their bikes to the park or the swamp. In middle school it was Friendly's all the way, and once eighth-grade graduation was over, The Ridge was home turf.

"Be back in an hour for dinner!" she called.

"Okay!" Evan grabbed his jacket off the staircase banister, ran out the front door, and hopped on his moped. The Ridge was about five minutes from his house, but since he spent the entire ride beating himself up about his negligence, it felt as if it took forever.

How could he have been such a loser? One minute he was thanking his lucky stars he had Patricia, and the next minute he was dissing her big time. She had almost made herself late for her game to comfort him, and then he hadn't even bothered to show up for her. She must hate him.

Evan pulled into the parking lot and searched the tall glass windows for familiar faces. He saw a few football players, but no one Patricia normally hung out with. He pulled off his helmet and started to swing his leg from the bike, but a loud group of kids burst through the double glass doors and he stopped midswing.

There was Patricia, still in her uniform. And Rider Marshall had his hand on the small of her back.

Evan sat back down on his bike—hard.

He watched, gripping the handlebars with his sweaty hands, as Patricia said good-bye to everyone and then smiled up at Rider. He led her over to his car and opened the door for her. Patricia stopped for a second and took a look around. Evan froze. She didn't see him.

Evan wanted to yell to her, but his heart was in his mouth. Did he really expect her to get out of that sleek, black car and hop onto his shabby bike? Would she really give up a ride with a popular, blond senior whom she'd had a crush on since the eighth grade?

Who am I kidding?

As Rider revved the engine and took off with Patricia, Evan slipped his helmet back over his head. Rider was a high-school god. And Evan was just a scrawny dork who couldn't even get his art shown. How could he ever compete?

For the second time that day Evan tried to make himself go numb, but it didn't work. As he turned the bike around and started home, he realized he'd never felt quite this much pain before in his life. He was starting to lose his girlfriend, and it was no one's fault but his own.

And maybe Rider's.

Patricia skipped up the steps to the porch and turned around quickly to wave at Rider, who was watching her from the car. It was all she could do to swallow a giggle.

Rider Marshall had driven her home! He'd bought her cheese fries and a chocolate shake and had played every song she requested on the jukebox and then had driven her home in his Mustang convertible with the top down and the stereo blasting. What a night.

Patricia burst through the door. Her parents hurried into the foyer from the living room. She grinned at her mom.

"I heard!" she said, hugging Patricia. "Congratulations on the shutout. I wish I'd been there."

"Thanks," Patricia said.

"And I heard you went out with Rider Marshall tonight," her mom added, stepping back. Her eyes shone with pride. Patricia suddenly had the sinking feeling that her mom was more excited about the fact that she went out with Rider than about her game.

"Did anyone call?" Patricia asked. Evan must have called, and it was time to remind her parents of her boyfriend's existence.

Her mom looked confused for a moment. "No. I thought you were out with all your friends."

Patricia looked at the floor. He hadn't shown up and he hadn't even called? She felt tears start to creep into her eyes, and she scuffed the floor with her cleat. "Not all of them," she said. "I'm gonna go get changed."

"After you get comfortable, come down and tell me all about it!" her mother yelled after her.

About the game or about the perfect senior boy who drove me home? Patricia wondered. At that moment she decided to lock herself in her room for the rest of the night. Her feelings about Rider and Evan were a huge jumble, and the last thing she needed was her mom's Evan-isn't-good-enough-for-our-daughter viewpoint.

She slammed the door behind her and threw herself onto her bed, staring at her Florida Marlins World Series poster. Usually just seeing the players' smiling faces cheered her up. But not tonight.

He hadn't even called.

This was depressing—and she shouldn't be depressed. She'd had a perfect game and an incredible night. Patricia reached over, grabbed a feather pillow, and hugged it to her chest. *Snap out of it,* she thought. *Think happy thoughts.*

Rider sitting in the corner of the booth near the window, his arm propped up on the vinyl seat back. The way the beaten leather band of his watch was melded to his thick wrist. The little golden hairs that stood out against his tan skin. The way his smile was so pure and his eyes scrunched up when he laughed. His perfect, clean, masculine scent.

Right around when her milk shake had reached half-mast, he'd unfolded his arm and laid it flat behind her so that if she inconspicuously leaned back just the tiniest bit, she could brush his skin with her hair—

Ring!

Patricia's eyes popped open. The phone. She flipped over onto her stomach, flailing her arms at the floor in the general direction of her telephone. She pulled it by the cord out from under a pile of T-shirts and grabbed the receiver. It had to be Evan.

"Hello?"

"Oh. My. Gosh. Patricia, you are such a lucky little—"

"Courtney?" Unless his voice had risen a few octaves and had taken on an early Valley Girl lilt, this was not her boyfriend.

"I'm kinda surprised you're there," Courtney continued. "I thought you and Rider might still be steaming up the windows."

Patricia rubbed her forehead with the back of her hand, feeling a tired sort of annoyance creep over her. "It's a convertible, Court. There's nothing to steam."

"Well, you could always give it the good old Buccaneer try." Her laugh was practically a cackle.

"Courtney, I don't *want* to kiss Rider. I haven't even *thought* about it," Patricia lied. Her subconscious had graciously served up the image during a particularly vivid dream the night before, and she'd spent much of her time in U.S. history class embellishing said dream in her mind. But Courtney didn't need to know that. Patricia's daydreams were her own business. "How many times do I have to tell you I have a boyfriend?"

"Blah, blah, Evan," Courtney blurted out. "Who came to your game looking all Armani and cheered you through a shutout? And who showered you with junk food and looked at you all night like you were God's gift to blond boys, making the rest of us ill?" She paused. "Has Evan even called you?"

"Of c-course . . . well, no," Patricia stammered.

"But he has a good reason. He was really upset about the arts festival this afternoon, and he takes these things really hard, and—" She stopped because she was sounding lame even to herself.

"Nice try," Courtney scoffed. As her friend rambled on about Rider's eyes, his intelligence, and his earning potential, Patricia found herself praying to the call-waiting gods. *Beep. Please just beep, and I will never abuse the *69 function again.*

"Patricia?" Courtney said suddenly. "Did you fall asleep on me or something?"

"Not quite," Patricia muttered. Her lips were half mushed into the pillow and her eyes were shut, but she hadn't been lucky enough to be overtaken by sleep.

Courtney huffed—she was the only person Patricia knew who could huff convincingly. "Fine. Just don't come running to me when you need advice on what to wear to Rider's fraternity functions next year." She sounded as if she actually expected Patricia to take this as a blow.

"I promise I won't," Patricia said, finally flipping onto her back and sitting up. "I'd better go." She paused as a monster head rush overcame her. "My bath beads are calling my name."

"I'll talk to you later," Courtney said. "But don't be surprised if Rider calls you before Evan. He'll probably want to ask if you enjoyed yourself tonight. One of those two guys *is* a thoughtful gentleman."

"Okay! Bye, Courtney!" Patricia hung up abruptly.

She put the phone down next to her on the bed and stared at the glittery butterfly stickers she'd covered it with when she was seven. It used to be the kitchen phone, but she'd inherited it after she'd taken it upon herself to decorate it. Patricia picked up the receiver to make sure there was a dial tone. There was. She slammed it back down and pushed herself off the bed.

Suddenly she felt as if she weighed about nine hundred pounds. She was crashing from all the excitement, and when her body crashed, it didn't mess around. And she still had five geometry proofs to write and half a Shakespeare play to decipher.

Patricia dragged herself to her closet, pulled down her plush blue robe, and headed for the bathroom.

Maybe Evan would call while she was soaking in the tub. Maybe her mom would bring in the portable phone and Patricia could chat with him until the water turned cold. Maybe he hadn't forgotten all about her.

She sat on the edge of the tub and turned on the tap, then dropped in some bath beads, squirted in the bubble-bath solution, and watched as the water formed into suds. She was too tired to even stand up and peel off her uniform, so she leaned back against the cool tile wall while the room filled with steam.

Patricia imagined sitting next to Rider at the diner, but this time none of their other friends were there. She would tell a joke, and he would laugh.

Then their eyes would meet, and the whole world would melt away, and he would lean in close to her. She would run her fingers through his soft, blond hair, and he would trace a finger down her cheek. Then she would close her eyes, and then—

Patricia's hand fell into the bathwater, and she jolted out of her daydream. The water was dangerously high, and she quickly shut off the faucet. Her heart was pounding. She blushed and looked around the empty bathroom as if someone were there, watching her—reading her thoughts.

As if *Evan* were there.

She looked toward the door, her thoughts of Rider fading away.

Her heart twisted with loneliness. Where was her mom with the phone? Where was Evan?

"Where are you right now, Patricia?"

Well, why don't you just call her and find out, brainiac? Evan told himself. He was lying on his back on top of his bed. He picked up a dart off his nightstand and threw it in the general direction of the dartboard—without moving a single nonarm muscle in his body. He missed the board by about three inches. Pathetic.

Evan pulled himself up and walked over to the dingy mirror that hung over his dresser. A photo of Patricia was stuck into the fake wooden frame around the glass—pushed in so that Courtney, who Patricia had her arm around, was mashed under the chipping plastic "oak."

"Okay, let's think about this," Evan said to the image of Patricia. "You're definitely mad at me for not showing up at your game. And you have every right to be. I was a loser. A thoughtless, useless, self-centered moron." He looked at his own reflection now. "But did you have to go home with that . . . that . . . senior?"

The movie reel started itself up in his head. He could practically hear the whir of the projector's wheels as it flipped on: Patricia sliding into the car with Rider, looking all giddy. The car screeching out of the parking lot, leaving solid black skid marks behind.

Maybe it wasn't as bad as Evan had thought it was. Maybe she hadn't been grinning. She'd just been working at a sesame seed stuck between her teeth, and that's why her lips were all pulled back. The Ridge was known for its sesame-seed-rife buns.

Sure. That was definitely it.

Evan popped a Zeppelin CD into his stereo, fast-forwarded to "Kashmir," and cranked the volume. His mom was out with friends, so he could wail on the air guitar as much as he wanted.

Only the musical spirit wasn't moving him, so he just flopped onto the beanbag chair in the corner and grabbed his sketch pad. He flipped it open and stared at a blank page as a familiar guitar riff ripped through his eardrums.

"I totally blew it," he said aloud. "I practically threw Patricia at that peroxide prince."

He picked up a piece of charcoal and drew a long, black line on the page. "Maybe she just got a ride home from him because they live near each other." He dropped back his head. "Maybe I'm just being an immature jerk and I should've called to apologize to my girlfriend hours ago, when I still had a chance of getting her to talk to me."

How stupid was he anyway? He could have figured out what to do about the arts festival after her game, but no, he had to take care of himself first. Instant gratification—one of his biggest weaknesses. And he could have sucked it up, gotten off his bike, and walked over to Patricia in the parking lot of The Ridge. She was his girlfriend. And he loved her. Maybe he couldn't say it, but that didn't change the fact that the thought of her being within five feet of Rider made his stomach want to vault up his throat, fly out his mouth, and make a run for the bathroom. Now that was love.

Patricia deserved an explanation. And an apology. And a big, fat kiss.

Evan chucked the sketch pad on the floor and crossed the room to pick up his phone. But on his way there he noticed the clock. It was way too late to call her. Even if she was still up studying or something, her parents wouldn't let him talk to her, and the late phone call would be one more black mark against Evan the-nightmare-who's-dating-our-daughter Schnure.

He wondered what the statute of limitations was on apologies and decided it was probably directly related to the magnitude of the crime. Flowers. Flowers would be key here. Hopefully post-home-room wouldn't be too late.

He'd get yellow roses. Her favorite. And compose something suitably ingratiating for the card.

That shouldn't be a problem since he felt like the scum of the earth.

SIX

"I'M SURE HE has a really good excuse for not showing up at the game," Isabel said as she dodged an illegal hall skateboarder Tuesday morning.

"How about for not even calling?" Patricia reminded her, stopping outside her homeroom and turning to face her friend. She hugged her binder to her chest. "Telephone technology is readily available to almost everyone nowadays," Patricia said.

"Well, at least you haven't lost your wicked sense of humor," Isabel quipped. "But still—"

"Hello, ladies!" Rider had come out of nowhere and was holding a stack of papers in front of each of their noses. "Could you hand these out in your homerooms?"

Patricia's heart was already pounding in her ears from his presence. Ugh! Why couldn't she just control her hormones?

"Uh, what are they?" she asked, taking the

papers from him. She noticed that her nails were all chewed up from the night before when she was waiting by the phone. She hid her hands, along with her binder and the papers, behind her back. Isabel shot her a "you've totally lost it" look.

"The tennis team is sponsoring a dance this weekend, and everyone needs to fill these things out," Rider said, holding up the rest of his forms.

"Computer love match?" Isabel read from the top. Her face was all skepticism.

"Yeah!" Rider was obviously excited by this whole thing. The energy just radiated from him. Patricia sighed. He couldn't have been cuter if he were a Gerber baby.

Imagine . . . a senior boyfriend . . .

"You answer a bunch of questions, and then we feed the forms into this computer and it spits out your perfect match," Rider explained. "Whoever you're matched up with is your date for the dance."

"You're kidding," Patricia said. "That's so cool." She risked bringing her hands out in the open to scan the pages. "Was this your idea?"

"I can't take all the credit," Rider said with a shrug. "They did it at my old school. It totally rocked." He started to back away. "I have to make sure all the homerooms have these, but I'll see you later."

"Okay, bye!" Patricia said, loving the fact that he wanted to see her later and that he went so far as to mention it.

"And hey, Patricia." He suddenly rushed back and stood right before her. Patricia stared into his picture-perfect face. "Fill it out wisely," he said with a wink. Then he grinned and was gone.

"Well, that was a hint if I ever heard one," Isabel remarked. The bell rang, and she patted Patricia on the back before heading across the hall to her class-room. "Good luck."

Patricia nodded. Her heart was still coming out of shock as she hustled into homeroom. She passed out the papers in a daze and fell into her seat.

Fill it out wisely. She replayed Rider's words in her mind. Was Isabel right about that being a hint? Did Rider want to go to the dance with her? Nah. Not possible. Surely some senior cheerleader like Belinda Barber had sunk her manicured nails into him by now. He was just messing around. Patricia almost laughed out loud at her own silliness.

The first announcement over the PA system stated that homeroom would be extended so that those who were interested could fill out the love-match questionnaires. Patricia grabbed a pencil from her backpack and set to work.

1. Your idea of a romantic evening is:
   a. An expensive candlelit dinner
   b. Dancing till dawn
   c. Watching the sun set
   d. A long hike and a picnic
   e. None of the above

Well, that was easy. She and Evan loved sunsets. Even though lately they hadn't gotten to see any for one handsome reason that should *not* be on her mind. Patricia filled in the little circle next to *c*.

2. Think of your favorite piece of furniture in your house. It's:

    a. A desk
    b. A bed
    c. A couch
    d. A chair
    e. Other

What an odd question. Had Evan written this thing? The thought made Patricia laugh. Her favorite piece of furniture was definitely the old rolltop desk that used to be her grandfather's. But she knew Evan worshiped his beanbag chair—he said it was the most comfortable place on earth. She filled in *d*.

It wasn't until Patricia got to number 20, favorite sport, that she thought of Rider again. There were about fifteen choices. Baseball, hockey, figure skating, tennis . . .

Fill it out wisely, he'd said. He'd winked. He'd smiled. Of course he wanted to get matched up with her. What other explanation was there? Patricia froze and began to sweat until her pencil started to slide around between her fingers. She glanced at the clock. There was plenty of time. Could she really do this?

Patricia started to erase. It wouldn't technically be her fault if the computer matched her with

71

Rider. It was a computer, not God. She started re-answering. 1. *a*. 2. . . . . Rider had told her he'd missed his bed when he was away at school, so she filled in *b*. She looked over her shoulder nervously, as if someone was going to catch her in the act. But she wasn't cheating—she was just manipulating an idiot form for a dance. That wasn't a crime, right?

Then why did she feel as if there were a spotlight blaring down on her and rabid attack dogs about to move in for the kill? *This is stupid. I am stupid,* Patricia thought. She was mad at Evan for being a less than perfect boyfriend, so she was sitting there trying to match herself up with someone else. Guilt can be such a fabulous wake-up call.

Patricia erased her answers again, started over, and responded honestly. Sunsets, check. Desk, check. Baseball, check. Who knew? Maybe she'd get matched up with some honors student from the junior class who she'd never even spoken to before.

The bell rang and Patricia quickly handed in her paper, trying to squelch her still lingering guilt.

At least now she knew whoever she got matched up with would truly be her ideal mate.

"Hey, man! Are those for me?" Lucas Rosen pulled one rose out of the bouquet Evan was holding and twirled it around between his fingers. "You shouldn't have."

"Quit it, man," Evan said, grabbing the flower back. He replaced it and then wiped his sweaty palm on his jeans as students began to meander out of Patricia's classroom.

He was just about ready to pass out from nervousness. The principal had announced Patricia's shutout over the loudspeaker during homeroom. Evan was insanely proud, but the fact that he'd not only missed a game, but a *huge* game, put him in even hotter water. Like scalding.

"I get it, dude. Nothing like a little early morning grovel, eh? All right, then. I'll leave you to it." Lucas picked up his skateboard and rested it on his shoulder, then turned to go. "Catch you in choir! And good luck!"

"Thanks a lot," Evan muttered.

"Are those for me?"

"Patricia! I didn't even see you come out!" Evan thrust the flowers toward her, and she took them carefully.

"Thanks," she said tentatively.

Evan swallowed hard. "You hate me, don't you?" he said as crowds of students walked around them. "I mean, it's totally cool if you do because if there's one thing I know about myself, it's that I'm eminently hateable. I'm the liver and onions on the dinner plate of life."

Patricia laughed and sniffed the flowers. Her hair fell forward, delicately framing her face. "I like liver and onions," she said, looking up at him through her thick lashes.

Evan studied her for a moment to make sure he'd heard right, then cracked a grin. Unreal. She

73

was going to give him a second chance. He tugged her arm and led her over to the wall so that people would stop tripping over them.

"Listen, Patricia, I'm really sorry." Evan leaned in close to her. "There's a card stuffed in there somewhere that explains how sorry, but don't read it until I bury my head in the sand."

She lowered her eyelids and looked down at the flowers. "It's okay."

He put his finger under her chin and lifted it up so that she would look at him. When Patricia's lashes finally fluttered open, Evan took a sharp breath. She looked just like an angel. An innocent, forgiving, loving angel in a blue denim shirt. "No, I mean, I'm *really* sorry," he said. "I should've been there for you, and it kills me to think that I let you down. You don't even know half the jerk I've been—"

Then he suddenly clammed up. He'd already decided not to tell her about The Ridge. He didn't want Patricia to know that he was too much of a coward to even approach her in Rider's presence.

She looked toward the door of her classroom and shrugged. "I don't know, Evan. I just think that part of being a couple is, you know, being there for each other, even if it's not always convenient."

Evan squirmed as the seriousness of her words sank in. He'd made her think she was inconvenient! A word he would never have equated with her. His life had gone from tolerable to incredible the moment she had become a part of it. Evan took her free hand in his, and she looked back at him. "I messed up," he told her. "And it's not gonna happen again. You're the best thing in my life. I want you to know that."

Patricia blushed and smiled. "Let's just forget about it, okay? We have to get to class anyway." She started to walk down the hallway, and Evan followed. "I know you had a rough afternoon yesterday, and there was no way you could've known that I'd play my best game *ever*."

Evan knew that was a well-deserved dig. He pushed open the heavy wooden door to the stairwell for her. "I heard you were amazing. Everyone was talking about it in homeroom. I swear I'll never miss another game."

"Well, then, I'll have to pitch another shutout just for you," Patricia said as they walked up the stairs together.

"I'm sure it'll be no problem," Evan replied with a lighthearted laugh. This had gone much better than anticipated. He dodged around her, taking two stairs at a time, and opened the next door for her as well.

"Thank you, sir." Patricia laughed too as she ducked past him into the upstairs hallway. Lucas, Max, and Isabel were waiting for them outside the rehearsal room.

"Yo, dude!" Lucas called, retying his blond ponytail. "Successful grovel, I see!"

"He kowtowed just the right amount," Patricia told them, handing her flowers to Isabel so she could smell them. Isabel took a sniff and then grinned at Evan.

"So what did you do all day yesterday while you were missing Patricia's Olympic-style pitching?" Isabel teased.

Max and Lucas laughed.

"Thanks, Isabel," Evan said.

"Sorry. Had to do it," she said, leading the group into the large, bright choir room.

"Actually, I came up with a plan to get my painting into the arts festival," Evan said.

"What do you mean, 'get it in'? I thought you just had to submit it," Max said, running his hand through his black hair.

"Here's the short version," Evan began, plopping into a chair and stuffing his backpack under the seat. "Mrs. Russo says the board of ed doesn't allow nudes to be shown in the arts festival, so she won't accept my painting."

"You did a nude?" Lucas asked. "Cool!"

Evan shot him a look. Lucas pulled an imaginary zipper across his mouth. "Anyway," Evan continued, "the board meets tonight, so I'm going to go and tell them exactly what I think of their stupid rules."

"All right, Evan. Damn the man!" Max said, slapping Evan's hand.

"I need you all to come," Evan said, making eye contact with each one of his friends. "And I need you to get whoever else you can to come too. We have to show them they can't strangle our freedom of expression just because we're not technically adults."

"I'm so there, dude," Lucas said, punching Evan's shoulder. "And the rest of the gang'll be there too . . . if I can pull them away from the Nintendo."

"What time does it start? Because if it's after practice, maybe we can get the whole team to come," Isabel chimed in.

"Eight. You'll have plenty of time," Evan responded.

As the group fell silent, Evan looked at Patricia, waiting for her to say something. She was the only one who hadn't given her promise of support yet. She looked back at him nervously, like a caged animal.

Evan felt something inside him shift. His confidence, possibly. "What?" he asked.

"I don't know. Do you really think this is a good idea?" She started chewing her thumbnail. "I mean, can't you just submit one of your other paintings?"

Evan stared at her, disappointment clouding his heart. "Patricia, you were there. You know this is totally unfair. And that painting is my best work."

"I know. I know," she said, glancing around the room as if she was looking for a way out. "I just . . . I don't think a confrontation is the best way to go."

Mr. Hageman walked into the room, and Evan stood up automatically for warm-ups. The other guys headed for the middle section of the risers, where they were supposed to be, but Evan didn't move. "I'm not talking about a confrontation," he whispered as everyone else took their places. "I'm not even gonna raise my voice unless they start acting like the closed-minded power freaks they are."

"See? That's what I mean! You're already hostile," Patricia whispered back, looking at Mr. Hageman out of the corner of her eye.

Evan didn't care if he slapped him with detention for not taking his place. At the moment he had to deal with the fact that his girlfriend seemed to be the only person who wasn't willing to support him.

He took a deep breath and let it out slowly. "Patricia, this is the only thing I can do. It's why I missed your game. I was busy finding out when the meeting was and how I could get in and get a chance to speak and everything. This means a lot to me. You just said we should be there for each other, and I know I'm not one to talk, but—"

Hageman started pounding out scales on the piano, and Isabel walked over to close the sound-proof door to the room, then moved into place behind Patricia, one riser up. Patricia swallowed and blinked up at Evan. Everyone around them started to sing. "All right. I'll be there. I'm sorry," she said. "If this is what you've decided to do, I'll come."

Evan was so grateful, he wanted to kiss her. So he did, on the cheek.

"That'll be enough of that, Mr. Schnure," Hageman said without missing a beat. "Why don't you put your mouth to a more productive use and sing?"

Evan grabbed his bag and rushed up the risers to join the other bass singers. As he stepped into place beside Max, Evan joined in the next scale.

This was going to be great. He was going to take a stand, and everyone was going to be behind him. So why wasn't he excited?

He glanced at Patricia back down on the floor level and realized he was still disappointed. She'd never really questioned his judgment before. Sure, when Evan had suggested she climb the school wall to watch the sunset, she'd balked for a second, but that was justified. This, he didn't get. She'd been almost as upset as he was at Russo yesterday. Why wasn't she with him on this?

Suddenly the answer hit Evan like a flash of light. Rider. Maybe Patricia was starting to catch the differences between Evan and the champion brownnoser. And maybe she was thinking that she'd rather have a dull but acceptable country-club boy than a guy who got into trouble . . . even if it was for fighting for what he believed in.

Evan suddenly felt sick to his stomach. He was beginning to wonder exactly what was going on between his girlfriend and Rider Marshall.

SEVEN

PATRICIA LEANED BACK in her creaky bedroom chair and massaged her temples, willing herself to relax. There was something she wasn't telling Evan, and it was making her moments-before-final-exams-caliber tense. And it wasn't something about Rider, although she *had* neglected to tell Evan about her evening out at The Ridge. She figured it wasn't that big an omission since other kids had been there—it wasn't as if it had been a date or anything. But that was beside the point.

She hadn't told Evan that she didn't want him to go in front of the board of ed that evening because she was afraid he was going to get in trouble. Sure, to an outside observer, talking reasonably with the powers that be might seem like the intelligent, mature, responsible thing to do. But she had a feeling there wouldn't be anything remotely mature about this encounter. Evan wasn't known for his subtlety, and it would be nice if he stayed out of jail, at least until after her birthday on Sunday.

Patricia stared at the two parallel lines intersecting the plane on the textbook page in front of her and told herself nothing was going to go wrong. After all, this day had been one big, good-karma party. First she'd been awarded a solo for the next concert during choir rehearsal, then the whole cafeteria had applauded for her shutout as she was standing in line for Tater Tots, and *then* the team had gotten out of practice early because Coach Cortez's sister had gone into labor. Patricia had arrived home in time to watch the *Felicity* tape her mom had recorded for her and do her homework before the board meeting. Surely, *surely* this streak of luck wasn't about to unstreak.

"Patricia! There's someone here to see you!" Patricia's dad yelled. She jumped up from her desk, grateful for the interruption, and ran to the front window. Rider's car was sitting in her driveway. Instant swoon. Unbelievable! More good luck!

Giddy with excitement, Patricia checked her hair quickly in the mirror, smoothed on some lip gloss with shaky hands, and walked slowly down the hall, not wanting to appear too eager. What was he doing here anyway?

At the bottom of the stairs Patricia peeked around the open front door. She was surprised, and actually a little disappointed, to find not only Rider, but Courtney as well.

"Hi, guys!" Patricia greeted them. "Come on in!"

"We were going to ask you to come out," Rider said. "We have to get some decorations for the dance and thought you might want to come."

Oh. Well, that invitation was fairly void of intrigue, but at least it explained why Courtney and Rider were hanging out. They were both on the tennis team, so obviously they were both working on the dance . . . and why did Patricia care anyway? Maybe Courtney and Rider could talk about their financial portfolios and fall madly in love over a perusal of their tax returns. Then Patricia wouldn't have to worry about her idiot dreams anymore.

"I don't know," she said, even though the thought of spending time with Rider was enticing—especially when he was wearing that T-shirt that hugged his chest in just the right way. "I have to be at the school at eight for Evan's big meeting."

Did Patricia imagine it, or did a shadow cross Rider's face when she mentioned Evan? Patricia was certain Courtney had rolled her eyes.

"We'll definitely be done by then," Rider promised. "I know exactly where to go."

"Come on, Patricia. It'll be fun," Courtney urged.

"You know you want to." Rider stared right into Patricia's eyes. All air was instantaneously sucked out of her lungs. She checked her watch, praying he couldn't see the sweat on her palms. Five-thirty. How long could decoration hunting possibly take? Some crepe paper here, a balloon or two there. Piece of cake. Besides, Courtney would be there, so it wouldn't be like Patricia was falling off the Rider wagon again. This was just a few friends hanging out. Well, Patricia and her friend, and the hottest guy who'd ever graced Patricia's front porch. "Okay. Let me just grab my bag."

"Great! We'll be in the car!" Courtney called.

Patricia jogged up the stairs and grabbed her purse off her desk. She took one more quick look in the mirror before running back downstairs and yelling to her parents that she'd be back soon.

That's weird, Patricia thought when she saw that Courtney was seated in the backseat of the Mustang. *Since when does she voluntarily give up shotgun?* Well, Patricia wasn't about to protest. She slid in next to Rider and slammed the door.

Rider grinned at Patricia, stopping her heart as usual, and revved the engine. She flicked on the radio to her favorite station, leaned back in her seat, and let her hair fan out behind her as Rider pulled out into the street. As she slipped her sunglasses on, she couldn't help thinking of how cool she must look, riding around in the front seat of a senior's convertible.

"So, where are we going?" Patricia asked, holding her hair back from her forehead so that it wouldn't whip into her eyes.

"Oh my gosh! I just remembered something!" Courtney exclaimed suddenly, leaning forward in her seat. "I have an English quiz tomorrow that I really have to study for!"

"Well, you guys said this wouldn't take that long," Patricia told her. "You'll have time later, right?"

Courtney laughed. "Patricia, you so don't understand. I didn't even read the book! And you know my notes are about as useful as calculus. I hafta go home."

"No problem," Rider said, hanging a left. "I'll just drop you off."

"Thanks!" Courtney said happily. She bounced back in her seat, and Patricia frowned. Since when was Courtney so psyched about studying?

Patricia didn't have a chance to ask since Rider screeched the car to a stop in the Sanderses' driveway about two seconds later. Courtney didn't even wait for Patricia to pop the seat forward. She climbed over the side of the car, straightened her shorts, and waved good-bye. "Have fun, you guys!"

"Later, Court!" Rider called. Courtney turned and jogged over to the front steps of her house. Patricia stared at the door for a minute after she'd disappeared inside, wondering what had just happened. She had somehow been suckered into the exact situation she was supposed to be avoiding. Alone time with Rider.

"So, Patricia," Rider began. She slowly turned to look at him. The racing of her heart argued with her logic. She knew she should figure out an excuse to go home, but her body's every impulse was urging her to stay. Patricia envisioned herself sliding across the seat and cuddling under his arm. He was so close. . . .

"Where do you wanna go?" he asked, pulling down his sunglasses and turning to look Patricia in the eye.

She could dive right into those eyes. She was suddenly aware of the fact that her thighs were stuck to the white leather seat. "I thought you knew exactly where to go," Patricia managed to say.

"I did," he said. "But now I'm more interested in you."

He couldn't have just said that. Not possible. Patricia's heart was in her throat. What could she say to that? "We're still talking about dance decorations here, aren't we?" she asked, barely even conscious of what she was saying.

The question hung in the air as a look of disappointment crossed Rider's face. Patricia wanted to just fade away and die. Rider had fed her the perfect line, and she'd passed. What was wrong with her?

"Sure, we are." He sat up rigidly and looked straight ahead. "What do you think, Great American Party Store or Party Box?"

Rider's tone was definitely forced. Patricia swallowed painfully. She'd just rejected Rider Marshall. Who did that? Had she hurt his feelings? Was he mad at her? She decided to use her usual tactic in the face of adversity—pretend nothing had happened.

"Party Box. Definitely," she chirped.

"Sounds good. You're just gonna have to help me with directions. There's a lot I still don't remember." He pulled the car out onto the road.

"Okay. Just get to Main Street, and it's easy

from there." They drove along in silence for a few minutes and Patricia stared out her side of the car, counting palm trees as they flew by.

Patricia desperately tried to think of something to say to ease the tension. She wished she could just rewind the tape and say something else, *anything* else, when he said he was interested in her. *I'm interested in you too,* she thought. Nah. Too lame. *Well, if you think* I'm *interesting, what do you think of this?* Then she could pull him to her and kiss him. He'd be surprised at first, but then he'd relax and there they'd be—making out in the front seat of his car and . . . Suddenly an image of Evan's face flashed before her, and she immediately felt ill. What was she thinking? She had a boyfriend. Sure, this was Rider Marshall. But she had a boyfriend!

Patricia wanted to be anywhere but here. Anywhere but sitting in uncomfortable silence with Rider, who was probably wondering what he was doing stuck with an infantile sophomore who couldn't even take a hint when it was shoved down her throat.

The car came to a stop. Red light at Main. She glanced timidly at Rider. He was actually smiling.

"Which way, Patty?"

A little shiver passed through her. She hated it when people called her that, but somehow when he said it, it was almost . . . sweet.

Patricia looked around. If she said right, she could get him to take her home—she'd tell him she had a headache or something. Then she could call Evan and repent for her impure thoughts. If she said left, they were on their way.

The light changed, and the guy behind them honked his horn.

"Patty?"

"Left," she said with a smile. "We want to go left."

Evan sat down in the front row of the orange plastic chairs that were set up auditorium style in the school cafeteria. Somehow, even though he'd known the meeting was going to take place here, he'd expected it to be all dark and menacing. He'd thought maybe they'd cover the cafeteria windows in dark cloth and set up those green library lamps on the tables to give the room an air of intimidating, scholarly seriousness.

But no. He faced a panel of nine parents who were seated behind the same bright white cafeteria tables he ate at every day. All the lights were on, and one of the panel members was even wearing a Hawaiian-print shirt.

Evan's friends sat behind him now—Max, Isabel, Lucas, and a bunch of other kids from art, choir, and the softball team.

Even with all the support, Evan was very anxious. He gripped his painting until his knuckles turned white. Patricia was among the missing, and without her here, he couldn't seem to get control of his nervousness.

He turned around to his friends and found Isabel staring at the door. She faced forward again and caught his eye, looking almost guilty.

"Where the heck is she?" Evan whispered, even though everyone else in the room was talking at normal volume.

"Somewhere that's not here," Lucas supplied. He sat Indian style on his chair, his denim shorts reaching past his knees.

"Thanks for the news flash," Evan said, more harshly than he'd intended.

Lucas's eyes widened slightly. "Feelin' the love in this room."

"Sorry, man. I guess I'm just a little, uh, worked up."

Isabel squeezed Evan's shoulder and gave him a reassuring smile. "She'll be here, Evan. She probably just had a hard time tearing her dad away from his computer to drive her over."

Evan nodded, but he didn't believe it any more than Isabel probably did. Mr. Carpenter didn't work past five as a golden rule—unless he was working on a big story for someone. And Evan knew for a fact that his most pressing job at the moment was a listing of summer concerts at the town bandstand. Not exactly research intensive.

The president of the board of education called the meeting to order, and Evan turned around in his seat, planting his feet firmly on the floor in front of him. He'd dressed for the occasion—wearing his only pair of loafers, khakis his mom had pressed for him, and a clean rugby shirt. He glanced at his mother out of the corner of his eye. She was standing by the wall where he'd planted her because he didn't want his friends to see him with mom support. She nodded at him discreetly and winked. Good old Mom. She knew enough to avoid giving him a thumbs-up or something equally embarrassing to mar his reputation.

"Good evening, everyone," the president said. "We'll start with a reading of the minutes." A nameplate in front of her read Margaret Green. She actually looked like a pretty nice lady. Her white hair was pulled up in a bun, and with her little glasses, she looked a bit like Mrs. Santa Claus.

Maybe this wouldn't be so bad after all. Evan settled back in his seat and silently went over what he wanted to say.

But as the meeting dragged on and Patricia still didn't show, Evan began to squirm. He checked the clock about once every twenty-two seconds. At eight forty-five his throat went dry and his stomach tied up like a pretzel. It was almost time for the board to open the floor to new business. *Please walk through that door, Patricia. Come on,* Evan thought. *Where are you?*

The door opened, and Evan turned . . . just in time to see the Burko twins' parents walk into the room. She wasn't coming. She hadn't approved of any of this in the first place. How could she do this to him?

"Evan Schnure?"

Evan reeled around, completely taken off guard. Margaret Green was surveying the small crowd.

"Here!" he said, raising his hand slightly. He'd spoken too loudly, and the word hung in the air over the audience. The president's eyes landed on him and she smiled.

"Hello, Evan," she said. "You're first on my list here. The floor is yours."

"Well—"

"Stand up," Isabel whispered.

Evan stood, kicking his painting over with a clatter. He nearly jumped out of his skin, but he recovered quickly and picked up the painting. *Don't lose your cool,* he told himself.

He cleared his throat, glanced at the vacant door one more time, and then began. "Well, ma'am, uh, I was told that I couldn't show my painting at the arts festival, and, to be honest, I really don't think it's fair."

"And who told you the painting was unacceptable?" Mrs. Green asked.

"My art teacher, Mrs. Russo," Evan said, holding the painting so that the back of the canvas was facing the board.

Mrs. Green made a note on the pad in front of her, then looked at Evan. "Well, we can't make a ruling on it unless we can see it, Mr. Schnure."

Evan glanced over his shoulder at Max and Isabel, both of whom did give him thumbs-up signs. He took a deep breath and turned over the painting. A couple of eyebrows raised and a few impressed expressions were exchanged.

Mrs. Green just stared. "Mrs. Russo was right, Mr.

Schnure," she said. "We can't let you show that painting."

Evan's heart dropped into his shoes. "Just like that?" he mumbled.

"I'm afraid so," she answered. "It's against school policy to show nudes in the arts festival."

"But I—"

"There are nudes in the art books in the school library!" Isabel exclaimed, standing up.

"Yeah, and whatever happened to freedom of expression?" Lucas shouted, jumping out of his chair.

"Next thing you know we're gonna be burning books!" Max joined in. A few of the kids in the audience applauded.

"That'll be quite enough from the peanut gallery," Mrs. Green said, growing stern. "Rules are rules, Mr. Schnure. And part of growing up is learning to live within the rules."

Evan's brain searched for an argument and came up with thousands. Rules were made to be broken was the most obvious. But he couldn't say anything—he didn't have it in him. He wanted Patricia there so badly. She hated being the center of attention, but she was always in control, knowing just what to say and how to act. And she always calmed him down.

But Patricia was a no-show, and Evan was at a complete loss.

"You may take your seats. All of you," Mrs. Green said.

Defeated, Evan fell into his chair. The painting

dangled between his legs, and he dropped back his head. This had to be the single most ego-shattering moment of his life. He'd been destroyed in front of a mass of his peers whom he'd invited for the show—and his girlfriend wasn't even there to support him. Evan felt his blood boil. Some girlfriend!

"Yep," Lucas said quietly. "Definitely feelin' the love."

"You have to be kidding!" Patricia exclaimed, laughing along with Rider. She couldn't believe she was sitting at The Ridge, having a normal conversation with her lifelong crush. Patricia hadn't stopped laughing for about ten minutes and was beginning to feel the workout in her abs. "Ten gallons of yogurt?"

"Yep! I couldn't believe it either. But Ben was a fund-raising fiend. The yogurt-a-thon was his idea, and he was going to make as much money as humanly possible," Rider explained through his own laughter. "Of course, a lot of the spectators probably wanted their money back when he puked."

"That's disgusting!" Patricia held her stomach and laughed some more, leaning back in her seat. Rider's so-called stuffy prep school sounded more like an amusement park than an astute academy. Patricia was beginning to wonder why he'd ever left.

"I know," Rider said, wiping his eyes and then popping a french fry in his mouth. "We were all lucky he made it to the garbage can."

Patricia fell into convulsions again. She was going to have to tell Evan this story later. It was classic.

Wait a minute—Evan. Patricia's eyes popped open and her laughter ceased. She sat up straight, said a quick prayer, and then looked at her watch. She practically swallowed her tongue. It was eight-thirty.

"Oh, no!" she wailed, jumping up from the table and scraping her leg on the edge. "We have to get to school—*now*."

Rider blinked up at her for a second and then rose slowly. Patricia was already through the door when she glanced back and saw him counting out money for the check. "Let's go, let's go," she muttered under her breath.

Outside, she rushed down the stairs. "I am so dead," she said loudly, earning a startled look from a little old lady who was walking inside. "So, so, so, so dead."

She jumped into Rider's car and looked around helplessly. He hadn't even emerged from the diner yet. She bit her lip and leaned on the horn. "Come *on*," she said through clenched teeth. He appeared at the door and hurried down the stairs and around to the driver's side.

"Patricia, I'm sorry," he said as he started the car. "I can't believe we lost track of time like that. It's my fault. You can tell him that." Rider threw the car into reverse and peeled out of the parking lot, heading toward school.

"It's okay. It's not your fault," she told him.

Or maybe it was. Who knew? He *was* the one who was just too starving to pass up The Ridge and had promised, promised, promised that he'd keep an eye on the time. Patricia rested her elbow on top of the door and leaned her forehead on her hand. What kind of excuse was that? She was capable of reading a clock. And it wasn't as if Rider had a stake in this meeting. It was supposed to be important to *her*. She was the one to blame. She'd been having such a good time with Rider—such a good time imagining he was her boyfriend—that she'd forgotten all about her *real* boyfriend.

"I am such a grade-A moron," she said under her breath. If Rider heard her, he didn't show it. "I mean, I was just complaining about how he missed my game and that we should be there for each other and blah, blah, blah. And now here I am, totally spacing on something that's more important to him than . . . than . . ."

She sat up in her seat as Rider blew by the turn they had to take to get to school.

"Where're you going?" she practically screamed.

"There're too many lights that way," Rider said. "I know a shortcut."

Patricia looked at him, then back over her shoulder at the sign for Prescott Road. A shortcut? She'd lived here her entire life and she didn't know of any shortcut this way. If Rider didn't even know how to get to the Party Box, how did he know a shortcut to the school?

She folded her arms over her chest and tried to figure out how to word her misgivings without sounding rude. She didn't want him to get mad at her. Suddenly the car jerked to a stop.

Rider swore and banged the heel of his hand on

the steering wheel. Patricia jumped and looked around. Old Bridge Way? He'd taken her to the godforsaken swamp? Everybody knew this street was a dead end. They'd all ridden their bikes here as kids to catch frogs and fireflies and get all muddy and sweaty. Rider had undoubtedly been part of that. How could he forget?

"I guess I don't know a shortcut," he said, throwing his arm on the seat behind her and turning around so that he could back up.

"Guess not," Patricia muttered. "Please, just go back. Fast."

"I'm trying," he said, cutting the wheel.

Patricia closed her eyes and told herself everything was fine. They'd be at the school any minute. What were the chances that Evan had been called on first?

"I can still make it," she told herself, blinking back tears. She fiddled with her watchband as if she could somehow hold back the time. "I can still make it." Rider shot her a sidelong glance, but she barely noticed. How could she have done this to Evan?

The school was coming into view, and there were a bunch of kids milling around outside. Patricia's leg was out the door before Rider had even pulled into a parking space.

She jumped out of the car, scanning the crowd for Evan. Her eyes fell on Isabel and she was about to ask what had happened when Evan came barreling through the front door, his painting under his arm. He did not look happy.

"Evan!" Patricia called out. Evan slowed halfway down the steps and looked at her. His clouded expression started to clear slightly.

Her heart hurt so badly, she suddenly realized that Evan was the only person she cared about. She could never feel this regretful, devastated, and desperate over anybody else. Not even Rider. Her arms ached to hold him.

"Patty!"

Patricia froze. Rider. She was still standing next to his car, the passenger-side door open behind her. She watched as Evan's face went ashen and his jaw dropped slightly. Obviously he'd just realized that Patricia had come with Rider. Rider walked around the car and stood at her side. "Everything okay?" he asked.

Evan blinked at her in disbelief for a second, then took off at Mach speed toward the far end of the parking lot. He didn't look back.

"Evan! Wait!" Patricia called. She brushed past Rider and chased after her boyfriend.

He was walking faster and faster, and her mind was reeling. What had happened in there? What was she going to say? *Sorry, honey, but I was out for a snack with this guy who everyone thinks I should dump you for?* That'd go over well. The guilt was crushing.

As Evan climbed onto his moped, Patricia realized that the first thing she was going to have to do was keep him from getting away.

She started to sprint. This, unfortunately, would probably be the easy part.

EIGHT

"GET OUT OF here, man. Just get out of here now," Evan told himself under his breath. Maybe if he talked out loud, he would stay focused and not throw a roaring fit, which was what he really wanted to do. Explosion was imminent. And he wasn't even thinking about the board anymore. The board was no longer an issue.

It was Rider. Patricia and Rider. How could she?

"Evan!" Patricia called.

Evan strapped his painting to the back of his bike. His mom had wanted to ride over with him, but he'd told her he'd want to be alone with Patricia after the meeting. Now he was just hoping his bike would be fast enough to get him out of here before his so-called girlfriend caught up with him. His girlfriend, Miss Let's-be-there-for-each-other-unless-Rider-presents-a-better-option.

"Evan! Would you please stop?" She was right

behind him now. He jumped on his bike, not even bothering with his helmet, started the engine, and reached for the throttle.

"Stop!" Patricia jumped in front of his bike.

Evan nearly jumped out of his skin. "Are you insane?" he screamed. "You trying to kill yourself?"

"If you would just listen to me for a minute, I wouldn't have to risk it," she said, staring him in the eyes with an expression of pure defiance. Where did she get off acting all high-and-mighty?

"Where've you been?" he asked.

She relaxed her stance a bit. "I lost track of time. I—"

"I'll bet," Evan blurted out.

"What's that supposed to mean?" she asked. "I'm trying to apologize here."

"Well, excuse me," Evan said. "I guess I was having a hard time seeing past your date." He looked over his shoulder toward Rider's car.

"He's not my date," Patricia said. "If you want to know what really happened, he and Courtney asked me to help them pick out decorations for the dance, but then Courtney remembered she had to study, so we dropped her off at home." She took a deep breath. "And then we stopped for a snack because we were starving, and I didn't realize how late it was. And *then* when I could still get here in time, we ran out of the diner and jumped in the car, but Rider took a shortcut—or what he thought was a shortcut, but it turned out to be a dead end, so we had to turn around." Another deep breath. "And we just got here."

For a minute Evan thought she might be making the story up, but a quick glance at her face and a clear sweep of his conscience told him better. Patricia wouldn't lie to him about something like this. She wasn't a schemer. But Courtney was. And Evan was convinced Rider was. He had a feeling he knew exactly how his girlfriend had ended up alone with Romeo.

He turned off his bike and leaned back slightly in the seat, balancing with his feet planted firmly on the ground. "Don't you see what's going on here?" he asked.

Patricia blinked a couple of times, obviously confused. "Going on where?"

"With Rider."

She rolled her eyes and opened her mouth to protest, but Evan interrupted. "Courtney was never going to go shopping with you guys. She set you up."

"She wouldn't do that," Patricia said a little too quickly. Evan could tell from the doubt in her voice that she had already suspected this might be the truth.

"And then," Evan continued, "Rider probably was the one who suggested food. . . ." Patricia looked at the ground, marking another correct guess.

"And when *you* figured out how late it was—it was you, right?" Evan asked.

Patricia nodded and started kicking at the ground. She stuck her hands in the back pockets of her shorts.

"Then Rider was in no rush to leave. So he took some so-called shortcut, making you just late enough to miss the meeting," Evan finished with a satisfied nod.

Patricia continued to kick at the ground for a few seconds. When she did look up, her eyes were shining with tears. Evan's breath caught in his throat. Oops.

"Are you done?" she asked quietly.

"Patricia—"

"First of all, Courtney *did not* set us up," she said defensively. "Second, I was the one who noticed the time, but it's not like Rider was thinking about it. He had nowhere to be." Her voice was gradually rising, and a tear ran down her cheek. "Third, Rider would never do what you're suggesting. He just didn't know where he was going. He feels like dirt because he made me miss—jeez, Evan, forget about all this stuff. What happened at the meeting anyway?"

Evan's heart was slamming against his rib cage. At first he felt bad about making Patricia cry, but somehow that last defense of Rider made him even angrier than before. She was defending the guy. Rider was moving in on her, and either she couldn't see it or she chose to accept it and even condone it. Evan couldn't take much more of this. He was fuming.

"You want to know how it went?" he spat. "It stank. It reeked. It was the worst single experience of my life. Does that make you feel any better about losing track of time?"

Patricia took a couple of steps back and pushed her hands through her hair, staring at a fixed point in space as if she was too stunned to focus on reality. "I can't believe you're acting like this."

"You can't believe *I'm* acting like this?" Evan demanded, starting his bike. Patricia's eyes were spilling over, and he began to feel like a complete jerk, but he couldn't stop himself. He was hurt, and that made him want to hurt her too. "You were the one lecturing me about relationships this morning, but you know what I just found out? I'm the one who's an inconvenience to you. That you can believe."

Evan saw the deep hurt crease her face. For a split second he wanted to fix everything—but he didn't know how.

Instead he took off into the night and didn't look back.

"Whoa, dude, you look like death warmed over!"

"Thanks, Lucas," Patricia muttered. "I feel so much better now."

"Sorry. Did you eat some bad eggs or somethin'?" he asked, falling into step beside her as she made her way to her locker.

It was one of those mornings when nothing she tried on fit right, everyone seemed to be staring at her, and every locker slam, gossip gaggle, and bell ring seemed louder and far more piercing than usual.

"No," she muttered, grabbing her lock and spinning it furiously. "I just had a hard time sleeping last night, that's all."

Lucas's head bobbed as if it were hanging from a Slinky. "I hear you. Wiggin' about the verdict, huh? That's a big bummer for Evan, I bet."

"I bet," Patricia repeated. She glanced at Lucas and felt her stomach turn. Normally she loved Lucas, but on mornings like this, she had no tolerance for his hyperness and positive attitude. And it was hard to accept that he had been there when Evan needed someone and she hadn't. Isabel had filled Patricia in on all the gory details last night, making Patricia feel even more worthless. She shoved some books into her backpack, slammed her locker door, and began to walk to class.

"Dude went down," Lucas said, following slightly behind her. "We tried to back him up, you know. But when that lady turned him down, it was like he sprung a leak, man. He just sorta—deflated." He made a little whistling sound and shrugged.

Patricia cringed at the vivid image. Instead of being an encouraging voice for Evan or even a shoulder to cry on, she'd been laughing it up with Rider. She was evil. Pure and simple.

"See you later, Lucas," she said halfheartedly, turning into her homeroom class.

"Later," he called after her.

She sat down, took a deep breath, and started to mull things over. She had to think rationally. The fact was, she had missed the meeting, but still, last night Evan could have at least told her what happened. If he had, she could have sympathized with him, held him, let him vent all over her. But he hadn't given her the chance. Not that she deserved it.

Patricia stared at the composition notebook on top of her binder until the little white-and-black pebbly design seemed to dance before her eyes. *I tried to apologize,* she told herself. *He wouldn't let me. He was completely out of control and irrational. It's not like Rider's a threat—not anymore.*

"Patricia! I saw you with Rider Marshall at The Ridge last night. You two looked *very* cozy!"

Patricia froze. Kari Matthews was standing over her with a scandal-hungry grin on her face. *Deny it. Deny everything,* she thought.

"Did you break up with Evan?" Kari prodded.

Patricia took a deep breath. This was bad. The gossip queen of Jamesport High had sniffed out a front-page-worthy headline. Patricia would have to treat Kari firmly before things got out of control.

"No, Evan and I did not break up," Patricia said calmly and slowly, her nerves playing Twister. "And we are not going to break up. Rider and I are old friends, and we were just talking."

"Oh, I see," Kari said with a knowing nod. A nod that indicated she completely did not see. A nod that showed she was forming her own conclusions.

Patricia grabbed the girl's skinny wrist before she moved away. "No, Kari. I'm not kidding. I'm not covering my butt. I'm not doing anything but telling you the truth." Patricia tried to make sure her eyes were clear and honest. One hint of pleading and Kari would assume she was lying, and the news would be all over the school before Patricia could blink.

"Okay. I believe you," Kari stated. "Could you let me go now? I bruise easily."

Patricia released her grip. "Yeah. Sorry." She sank back down in her seat again as Kari flitted on to her next victim.

This was horrible. People were starting to talk. And she knew that if someone had seen Evan out with some other girl and assumed it was a love thing, she'd be swimming in a puddle of tears right now. Maybe she wasn't technically cheating on him, but she wasn't being fair to him either—not in her actions and definitely not in her thoughts. She had to grow up. She had to honor her promise to herself and stay away from Rider.

"Listen up, everyone!" Mr. Brendon said, calling the room to attention. He had a grin on his face a mile wide. "It's love-match time," he announced, wagging his eyebrows comically. A general murmuring swept around the room. "Get ready to find out who your lucky dates will be for the big dance. I'll pass them out individually so that the results will be private." Mr. Brendon started to walk up and down the aisles, handing out little pink strips of paper.

Patricia fiddled with her pen as she watched each slip pass from hand to hand. She saw her classmates grinning, or blushing, or rolling their eyes. One girl shrieked, and everyone laughed.

Suddenly there was a pink square facedown on her desk. Patricia just stared at it.

"Aren't you curious?" Mr. Brendon asked. "It's your one true love."

Patricia glanced at him, managed a half smile, and then slowly slid the paper to the edge of her desk. She flipped it over and read the name.

Then she read it again, closed her eyes, opened them, and read it again.

Suddenly her forehead was lying flat on her notebook and her mind was repeating four small syllables over and over again.

Rider Marshall.

What was she going to do with that?

NINE

FROM THE TOP riser Evan focused every last ounce of his telepathic energy on the back of Patricia's head. *Turn around. Come on. You know you want to.* Not that he *had* any telepathic powers, but there wasn't much else he could do to get her attention in the middle of choir practice.

"Mr. Schnure. Will you be singing anytime soon?" Mr. Hageman asked as the rest of the group continued with the song. Evan hadn't even realized he'd stopped. He glanced at Patricia and saw her shoulders tense, but she didn't turn to look at him. Evan opened his mouth and joined in.

This was out of control. First she'd ducked into class late and not even glanced in his direction. Then, when he started to walk down the risers toward her, she'd bolted for the bathroom and hadn't come back until after warm-ups had started. This was not a good sign.

Evan knew he'd crossed the line from moderately obnoxious to full-blown butthead last night. And he wasn't proud of it. But it was his pride that had forced him to do it in the first place. Every time Patricia had defended Rider and his obviously ulterior motives, it had been like a knife to Evan's already unsure heart. Why did there have to be seniors anyway?

After a night of examining his conscience, Evan was ready for another round of explanation and apology. It was like a game show. "Our next contestant laced into his girlfriend in a public parking lot in order to cover a bruised ego. Evan Schnure, come on down!"

Evan was still irritated and a little insulted that Patricia had missed the meeting, but he believed that she hadn't done it intentionally. And he was attempting to remove Rider from the equation. It wasn't easy to forget the image of her showing up with his newly anointed nemesis, but Evan realized that if Patricia had been out with Isabel and lost track of time, he wouldn't be as upset. It really wasn't fair to hold her choice of company against her, as long as she wasn't interested in Rider—which she had said she wasn't.

When it came down to it, Evan had missed her game and Patricia had missed the meeting, so technically they were even. It had to make them even because these awkward morning makeups had to stop. He'd grown tired of being one half of a drama couple these past three days. He wanted to go back to being fun-loving Evan. He *missed* fun-loving Evan.

The bell rang, and everyone grabbed their stuff. Evan rushed to get to the door before Patricia. He slid in front of her, grabbed her books out of her hands, and smiled. "I hold these for ransom until I get an acknowledgment of my existence."

Patricia raised one eyebrow. "What, no flowers?"

"The way I see it, *you* owe *me* flowers," he said, balancing her binder on one finger. He had this habit of getting manic when he was on the spot.

"Really?" She snatched her binder back but didn't make a move to leave.

"I missed your game and brought you flowers, so you missed my meeting and I figure that means you owe me flowers."

"I'll have to think about that one," Patricia said. Then she smiled. Encouraging. "Can I have my other book back now?"

"Not until you say you owe me flowers," he said, holding the book high.

Patricia hugged her binder against her chest. "Okay, maybe . . . but first you have to apologize for the little screaming session I endured last night." Her blue eyes clouded over.

Evan surrendered the composition book. "Patricia, I'm really sorry about that," he said as she shoved the notebook inside her binder and avoided his eyes. "I was just venting. I mean, you obviously caught me at a bad moment."

"Obviously," she repeated quietly.

Evan's heart turned in his chest. He reached out and tucked her golden hair behind her ear. Just touching her made his heart ache even more. "I don't know about you," he said. "But these emotional one-on-ones are getting old for me real fast."

Patricia nodded. "Me too. I'm really sorry I missed the meeting, Evan. You have no idea how sorry."

"I guess you heard what happened," he said. He took her backpack from her and swung it over his own shoulder. Patricia nodded solemnly. "Can I walk you to class?" Evan asked.

"Sure," she answered. Evan followed her out the door and down the hall toward the history wing. "So, what're you going to do now?" she asked, stealing a glance at him.

"I don't know," he answered quickly. He wasn't going to tell her what he had planned for the arts festival. He knew she'd try to talk him out of it, and the way he saw it, he had no other choice. "Can we move on to the next topic? I'm still kind of freaking about the whole thing." That was the truth. Evan's self-respect was on the critical list.

"Sure, I understand," Patricia said. They had reached her classroom, and she took her backpack from Evan. Then she gave him a little half smile. "C'mere," she said, standing on her toes. Evan leaned down, and she wrapped her arms around his neck, kissing his cheek. "No more fighting," she whispered in his ear.

Evan closed his eyes and held her tight. "No

more fighting," he agreed, his heart squeezing. She was so ridiculously sweet.

"Get a room!"

Patricia sprang away from Evan. He looked up to find Courtney breezing past them into Patricia's history classroom. Evan laughed. "Here's a change of subject for you," he told Patricia. "Guess who I got matched up with for the dance."

She paused and blushed slightly. "Uh, who?" she asked.

How cute—she was worried. "No need to be jealous, trust me," Evan comforted, digging in his back pocket for the paper. He uncrumpled it and held it out for her to see. "Courtney Sanders," he stated.

Patricia grasped the paper, her eyes widening in shocked silence. Then she cracked up. Evan laughed along with her, grateful for the release.

"That computer must have a virus the size of Miami," Patricia said, laughing even harder. "I bet it couldn't match Superman with Lois Lane."

"Seriously," Evan said. "Who did you get?"

"Strangest thing," she said with a giggle. "I, uh . . . I didn't get matched with anyone. I guess I'm not love material."

Evan smiled. "I wouldn't say that."

Patricia blushed deeply this time, and their eyes locked. Evan struggled to find his tongue. Love material. Of course she was love material. *Just tell her you love her, idiot.*

"Patricia, I—" The first bell rang, and he

jumped. "I gotta go," he said, turning and starting to jog down the hall. He was half relieved and half irritated at himself. Why couldn't he just say that he loved her? Well, that wasn't exactly the best moment to tell her. Suddenly an idea hit him. He stopped and spun around. "Hey, Patricia!"

She had just disappeared inside the classroom, but she stuck her head back out. "Yeah?"

"Do you want to have dinner tonight?" he yelled to her.

She smiled broadly. "I'm all yours!" she called back.

Evan heard groans from inside the classroom, but he didn't care.

"That's what I like to hear!" he said.

"I have this burning desire never to go back to school . . . or home . . . or . . . anywhere, really," Patricia said, stretching out on her back in the rapidly cooling sand. "Whoever had this picnic idea must've been a genius." She smiled and closed her eyes, folding her arms behind her head.

"My girlfriend the genius," Evan said. "So glad you talked me out of the fancy, expensive restaurant scene. What was I thinking?"

Then Patricia heard a little squishy noise and felt something wet on her nose before she could defend herself.

"Hey!" She sat up, opening her eyes and wiping the wet lump with the back of her hand. She came away with a blob of whipped cream.

Evan jumped to his feet, laughing. He started to

back up but stepped on his overlong jeans with his heel and fell backward. For a split second Patricia thought about going for the Reddi Whip bottle in his hands, but her eyes fell on the cooler near her feet and she got a better idea. She reached forward, grabbed a can of Sprite, and shook it hard.

Patricia saw realization dawn in Evan's eyes.

"It's payback time!" she cried. She bolted up as Evan started to scramble to his feet, but he was a moment too late—Patricia popped the top and showered Evan with Sprite. Little beads of silvery liquid caught in his hair as he slowly stood. Then he just closed his eyes and took his punishment until the can had stopped spewing.

"Are you done?" he asked, keeping his eyes closed.

Patricia frowned, confused and disappointed. "Well, that was no fun. You're supposed to scream and flee and . . . stuff." She tossed the can onto the big beach blanket and shrugged.

"No. I think I'd rather . . ." Evan's eyes opened, and he grinned menacingly. "Hug you."

"Don't you dare!" Patricia screamed. Evan lunged for her, engulfing her in his sticky arms. She felt little patches of wetness all over her arms and face. "Ugh! Let me go!" She laughed hysterically, struggling to break free.

"I don't give up that easily," Evan said, laughing as well. "You should know that about me by now."

Patricia stopped squirming and looked Evan directly in the eyes. "Bet I know how to make you let go," she challenged.

"Really?" he asked, raising his eyebrows. "I'd like to see you try."

"Okay." Patricia kissed his chin, and then his neck, and then his cheek. His hold started to loosen, and she felt his breathing quicken. She reached up and slid her hand up his shoulder and around his neck. He kissed her forehead and then trailed little kisses down her cheek until their lips were nearly touching.

"See?" she said. "It worked." Her heart was pounding, and every inch of her skin tingled as a breeze skittered across the deserted beach.

"You're very talented," he said huskily.

"I know," she said. She pushed herself up onto her toes and kissed him on the mouth. It took him a split second to react, but then his lips moved against hers, and Patricia lost herself in Evan. In his warmth, his taste (back to spearmint), his smell. Ah, bliss.

She couldn't believe she'd ever thought of kissing Rider.

Rider.

Patricia slammed back down to earth with the force of a comet. How could Rider pop into her mind at a time like this? Her knees jellied.

"Hey. Are you all right?" Evan asked, holding her shoulders. "You suddenly look . . . not good."

Patricia felt sick to her stomach. "I'm fine," she said. "I just got a little dizzy." She sat down on the blanket and closed her eyes, hoping to hide the guilt.

"Yeah, well, I have that effect on girls," Evan teased, sitting down next to her. "Do you want anything?"

Patricia looked around for something to focus on. "You know what? Maybe I didn't eat enough. Do we have any more chicken?" She was completely stuffed, but she had to think of something.

Evan scrounged through the picnic basket, tossing aside a few Saran Wrap wads. "Negative," he answered finally. "How about an apple? I'll even peel it for you."

"Perfect," Patricia said quickly. Suddenly she couldn't be near Evan any longer. Just being close to him was compounding the guilt she felt over her thoughts, over the fact that she'd missed Evan's big night because of Rider, over the fact that she'd lied to him that morning about her computer love match. "I think I'm gonna go down by the water," she said, pushing herself up.

Evan glanced up at her. "Okay. Be right there." He picked up a knife and started to carefully peel an apple. Patricia tensed at his attentiveness. Guilt. Guilt. Guilt. She turned and walked toward the crashing waves.

When she hit the dark, damp sand at the edge of the beach, she stopped and drew a heart in the ground with her toe, letting out a loud sigh.

She stared out at the waves as dusk started to darken the sky and thought back on the time she'd spent with Rider. Her overall feeling about him wasn't mind-blowingly rosy. Sure, she'd felt cool hanging out with a senior. She'd been high on the fact that her friends were jealous. And she'd blushed and grinned over his attention. But being around

Rider made her . . . tense. She always felt that she had to perform for him—she had to be cool and smart and sophisticated.

It's not worth it, she suddenly realized. *If I'm with Rider, I can't be myself and I have to lie to Evan. Rider just isn't worth it.*

"An apple for the beautiful lady?" Evan wrapped his arms around her from behind and held a freshly stripped apple in front of her mouth.

Patricia grinned. "The last time a beautiful lady accepted an apple, she ended up catatonic."

"Live on the edge. I don't see seven little dwarfs running around."

"Can't argue with that logic." Patricia took the apple and bit into it.

Evan held her around the waist and rested his chin on her shoulder. "Aw, look! You drew a little heart. Is that for me?"

Patricia nodded and swallowed. "Of course it's for you." She reached out with her foot and drew an *E* and an *S* over the heart. This was where she belonged—she was sure of it. She could always be herself with Evan. Even when he was challenging her to do new things, she never felt that she was changing for him. She just felt that she was really living—excited, happy, and carefree.

Evan squatted down and wrote in a *+ PC* after her *ES*.

ES + PC. That was the way it should be. And Patricia felt sort of . . . proud.

She wasn't going to that dance with Rider. And if

they wanted to make her go with someone other than her boyfriend—other than the guy she loved—then she wasn't going at all.

"This one. This is the one that'll win me the championship," Evan said dramatically, holding up a smooth, oval rock about the size of a jawbreaker. He'd managed to find the perfect rock in the not so strong light coming from the parking lot at the top of the beach. The moon was full too, which helped. He turned the rock between two fingers, inspecting it as if it were a diamond.

Patricia shrugged. "Well, if you think you can take me, Patricia 'Shutout' Carpenter, with that second-rate rock, all I have to say is, doubtful."

"Doubt*less,* you mean," Evan replied. He pulled his arm back to the side and flung the rock as hard as he could out over the waves. Patricia put her hands above her eyes like a sailor and looked at the water. The rock disappeared in the dusk. Her eyebrows scrunched up.

"That was pretty darn far," she said.

"Winner and still champion," Evan declared, throwing up his arms Rocky style.

"You are the master," Patricia joked, getting down on her hands and knees in the sand and bowing her head to him.

Evan grinned, finding it hard to believe he could be this giddy over a rock-throwing contest. But he knew that wasn't all it was. He was downright slaphappy over the fact that he and Patricia were together. Alone. Relaxed.

He held out his hand in front of her face. "You may kiss the royal hand," he said, thrusting his nose in the air. Patricia leaned forward and bit him.

"Ow." He pulled his hand back and shook it, laughing. "You'll pay for that one," he warned, dropping into a wrestler's crouch and preparing for battle.

"No! No! I can't take any more wrestling or food fights or anything," Patricia protested, climbing to her feet. "Can I make it up to Your Royal Rock-Flinging Highness if I take a picture of this most glorious moment instead?"

"You brought a camera? Does it have a flash?" Evan asked, standing up straight. Patricia nodded. "Why didn't you say so? Where is it?"

Patricia smiled. "It's in the side zipper pocket of my backpack." She started walking up the beach toward the blanket.

"That's okay. I'll get it!" Evan offered. He ran up the beach, kicking up sand behind him. Yep, this was just the kind of time to record on film. One of those cool, normal yet fun evenings he and Patricia might forget a year from now, but if they had a picture, he could flip to it and say: "That was the day, you know, with the whip cream and the Sprite?" And they would laugh.

Evan dropped to his knees next to Patricia's bag. A year from now. He was surprised he'd had that thought. He never thought that far ahead. He looked over his shoulder at Patricia. She was walking along the edge of the water, letting the waves lap at her slim ankles. Her hands were behind her back, and she was concentrating on her feet as she walked.

Her golden hair billowed back behind her, and the intent look on her face was so precious. He focused on her for a moment and tried to freeze that moment in his mind. The curve of her cheek. The moonlight in her hair. The sand on her toes. He wanted that mental picture in his memory forever.

Patricia looked up, breaking the spell. "What's wrong? It's there, right?"

"Yeah, just a sec!" Evan called, smiling and turning back to her bag. He unzipped the pocket and didn't see anything but a bunch of pens and a lipstick. He opened the main part, and a piece of paper caught in the breeze. Evan yelped and grabbed it before it blew away, but when he went to shove it back into her bag, he paused.

It was a little pink slip of paper—just like the one from the computer matchup that morning.

Evan glanced at Patricia, his hands shaking. She was looking out at the waves. He unfolded the paper quickly and read the name. He felt his heart turn cold and shivered as the wind hit him with a gale force. This couldn't be. She'd told him she hadn't been matched. But there was her name at the top, and there it was in block letters:

YOUR DATE FOR THE LOVE MATCH DANCE IS: RIDER MARSHALL

TEN

"HEY! PATRICIA, IT'S Rider!"

Patricia shrugged out of her jacket as she listened to the confident, cheerful voice on the answering machine. She smiled slightly and flung her jacket on one of the wooden kitchen chairs as she crossed the room to the refrigerator.

"So, I have this little piece of paper that says you're my date for a certain dance . . . ," the voice continued.

Patricia pulled out the orange-juice carton and grabbed a clean glass off the plastic dryer next to the sink. She noticed her knees were bopping to her own mental beat as she poured the juice, and she laughed.

". . . but I wanted to ask you officially, so . . . be my date?"

Patricia paused in mid-OJ swig. He sounded so

119

psyched . . . so . . . sure. She felt kind of bad that she was going to have to say no.

"555-2292. Call me." The machine clicked off. Patricia took a deep breath and shrugged. Rider was just going to have to move on to the next girl. Heaven knew there were scads of salivating sweeties just waiting for Rider to bless them with a blink in their direction.

Laughing again, Patricia grabbed her backpack from the floor where she'd tossed it and reached inside. Her fingers closed around the pink slip of paper. She crumpled it up, walked over to the garbage can, and tossed it inside.

She and Evan were going to break the rules and go to the dance together.

They hadn't actually discussed it, of course, because when Patricia was about to bring up the subject at the beach, Evan had suddenly cried stomachache and had driven her home. It was rather abrupt. One minute he was messing around with her in the sand, and the next he looked about as healthy as a beached whale. But eating almost an entire chicken could do that to a person.

Patricia rinsed out her glass, then walked over and grabbed the portable phone from her mother's cluttered desk. Might as well get it over with.

As she dialed Rider's number, her heart started to pound. She'd never actually called the guy before. And she wasn't only calling him to say hi; she was calling him to turn him down. Her eighth-grade self was banging her head against the flowered kitchen wall.

The line started to ring. Her eighth-grade alter ego would just have to smarten up. So what if he was perfect? He wasn't the guy Patricia wanted. Not anymore.

"Hello?"

Here goes. "Hi, Rider?"

"Patty? Hey! I was wondering when you were going to get around to calling."

Patricia stared at the floor and started walking around the kitchen on her tiptoes, touching only the blue tiles with her feet—a kitchen-phone conversation habit. "Yeah, well, I was out with Evan," she said.

Good opening, she thought. *Bring in the boyfriend.*

There was silence on the other end. "Oh."

"Listen." Patricia walked around in a tight circle on four blue squares. "I can't go to the dance with you."

"But those are the rules of the dance," Rider said. Was that a bit of a whine? Nah. Seniors didn't whine.

Patricia stopped and grabbed hold of a counter ledge. She'd made herself dizzy. "I know, but Evan and I really want to go together," she explained, closing her eyes. *Just let it go,* she begged silently. "I hope you understand."

There was an inordinately long pause. "Sure. Sure, I understand," Rider responded, sounding a little distant.

"I'm really sorry." Patricia wished she were more eloquent.

"Me too," Rider answered.

"Right, well, I'd better go," she said, tapping her hand against the counter nervously.

"Okay." Rider took a deep breath. "Patricia, you're gonna change your mind."

"What do you mean?"

"Just that you're gonna change your mind."

Okay, now this was getting weird. "Right. Well, good-bye."

"Bye!" She hit the off button and replaced the phone in its cradle. She stared at it for a second as if it could clue her in to that last bit of conversation.

"Nothing's gonna make me change my mind," she said out loud as she swept up her backpack. "Evan is the only person I want to go to this dance or any dance with."

"Dude, maybe she spaced. Chicks are like that sometimes," Lucas suggested.

Evan rolled his eyes. "Keep your voice down, man," he whispered. His back was pressed up against the school bathroom wall, and his legs were sprawled out in front of him. His banned painting lay at his side. "Jeez, I'm sorry I even told you."

"Sorry," Lucas said, plopping to the floor next to Evan. "I was just trying to help. You're the one who's wiggin' over something that means nothing."

Evan looked at Lucas incredulously. "She *lied* to me," Evan said. "That's not nothing."

"Well, you lied to her about what you were doing after school today," Lucas pointed out, pulling a blue ski mask over his face.

"I did not lie; I just didn't tell her . . . and what the heck is that for?" Evan demanded, gesturing at Lucas's headgear.

"In case anyone sees us," Lucas answered through the little mouth hole.

"Take it down a peg, secret-agent man. This isn't *Mission Impossible*."

"Do you want my help or not?" Lucas asked, pulling the mask back off.

"Yeah, I want your help," Evan admitted.

"Then let me have my fun." Lucas's brown eyes were twinkling. "And if you ask me about Patricia—which you did, by the way—I think the girl was just protecting your fragile male ego. If you think she's gonna dump your sorry butt, you're reality impaired. The chat around the caf is that she is one hundred percent, prime time in love with you." Lucas slapped Evan on the back and pulled his ski mask back over his face.

Evan knew that comment should make him feel better, but it didn't. He couldn't get rid of his feeling that Patricia wanted to go to that dance with Rider. Who wouldn't? Rider was a popular, wealthy senior with a car, who'd never been in trouble in his life. Evan was certain that Patricia was just waiting for the right time to tell Evan it was over—so he was avoiding her like crazy. Today he had pleaded his way out of the choir field trip, claiming laryngitis.

Evan told himself that there was no use in avoiding the inevitable, that he should take it like a man. There was just one small problem—he was totally in love with Patricia and scared to death of losing her.

The lights went out, and Evan's heart jumped.

"Show time!" Lucas whispered, rubbing his hands together. He grabbed a flashlight and flicked it on.

"Let's do it," Evan said. He grabbed his painting as Lucas silently pushed open the bathroom door and looked both ways. He waved Evan out, and Evan shook his head but kept his mouth shut. If Lucas wanted to be dramatic about it, who was Evan to judge?

Evan followed Lucas and the bouncing beam of light silently through the cafeteria and out the doors that led to the lobby. They looked around, but the place was deserted. Set up in the spacious entryway were dressing-screen-style display walls. Exhibits from the art classes were hung on the walls—set up for the next day's arts festival. Evan walked right over to the center display. If he was going to make a statement, he might as well make it loud and clear.

Lucas stood behind him. "That's it, man; go for the throat."

Evan leaned his painting against the display and reached up to unhook a silk screen. Lucas unhooked the pastel next to it, and they each moved them aside. There was just enough room to hang his work in the center. While Lucas replaced the nameplates beneath the other projects, Evan hung his painting, then stepped back to admire his handiwork.

"Perfect," he said with a nod. "It's the focal point of the room."

Lucas sidled over and stood next to Evan. "Aces, Evan. You are the man."

Evan chuckled. "Thanks, Luke. Shall we?"

Lucas pulled the ski mask off and twirled it on one finger. "That was too easy. I was looking forward to a little intrigue and possible personal injury."

"Sorry to disappoint," Evan said. "Oh! I almost forgot." He pulled a homemade nameplate out of his pocket and pinned it to the display beneath his painting. "If you're gonna do it, you might as well do it right."

Evan led Lucas back to the cafeteria, unlocked one of the tall windows, and slid through. Easy as pie. Once Lucas had made it through, Evan pulled the window as near to closed as he could get it.

"So, are you going to call Patricia tonight?" Lucas asked as they walked toward the side street where they'd parked Lucas's truck.

"No. I don't think so," Evan replied. He knew he really should. He should warn her about the painting—that the powers that be were probably going to be waiting to snag him in the morning. But as he thought that over, a wave of dread washed over him. And it began to press down on him like a lead blanket.

Suddenly Evan had a sickening vision that

Patricia would be standing in the lobby the next day with Rider and Courtney, talking about what a stupid maneuver he'd made. Then she'd turn to Evan and tell him that she didn't really appreciate his stunt and would rather date a nice, responsible guy like Rider.

Evan's guts were tied in a knot by the time he climbed into the passenger seat of Lucas's RAV4.

"You okay, buddy?" Lucas asked as he started the engine. "Your face is totally drained. It's like a blood-free zone."

"I'm cool," Evan managed to say. "Let's just go."

Evan concentrated on breathing as Lucas drove. In through the nose, out through the mouth. He'd never hesitated for a moment about adding his painting to the show. He knew what they'd do to him—detention for a week, maybe a suspension. Nothing he hadn't experienced before.

But he'd been so separately focused on Patricia's computer-matchup lie and the painting plan that he hadn't really thought about how the two issues could entwine. Now he could see it as clear as day. He'd just given Patricia the perfect opening line for her breakup speech.

Evan sank lower into his seat and stared at the gray ceiling of the car, hoping he could make it home before having his imminent nervous breakdown.

Reality impaired. Who knew Lucas could be so intuitive?

ELEVEN

"HE'S DEAD. WE might as well just go dig him a grave," Max said from the center of the crowd that had gathered around Evan's surprise exhibit Friday morning.

"Max! Stop saying that!" Patricia snapped. She felt as if she were waiting in line for the Psycho Scream roller coaster. The vice principal was practically salivating as he policed the front door, waiting for Evan to show, and half the school was gathered, waiting for the first public execution in Jamesport history.

"It's really quite good," Mr. Flank, her English teacher, remarked to another teacher. "It shows an incredible maturity." The irony of that statement wasn't lost on Patricia. The painting might have a mature sensibility, but Evan's stealth mission was one of the most childish stunts he'd pulled to date. Why did he do things like this when he knew he

127

was going to get in trouble? Did he *like* being in trouble?

"Maybe he's not gonna show," someone said.

"No, he'll show," another guy answered. "You can't pull something like this and then not show up to take the credit. He'd look like a gutless wonder."

Patricia couldn't take it anymore. She needed to breathe. She shoved her way through the front door and out into the fresh air. Since when was it so unbelievably hot? She pulled off her blue cardigan sweater and tied it around her waist and she was still hot.

Anger. It must just be anger. Patricia had called Evan twice the night before to see if he was okay since he hadn't been on the choir trip. He'd never called her back, and now she knew why. He was probably afraid he'd blab about what he'd done with his painting and knew Patricia would lose it.

She scanned the parking lot, looking for Evan's bike. She had to intercept him and warn him about the lynch mob. Maybe he really wasn't coming. Maybe he'd simply suffered from a bout of insanity and was resting after a night of therapy. Patricia caught a flash of light reflecting off something in the parking lot and jumped. It was Evan's helmet. She started to jog. She was panting with nervousness and anger by the time she reached him.

"Evan!" she said, coming up behind him and grabbing his arm as he removed his helmet.

Evan jumped. "Are you trying to kill me?" he asked.

"No. But they are!" she said, throwing her arm out toward the school. Someone must have seen her bolt because the crowd was starting to filter out onto the steps. One of the librarians was trying to herd the students inside while the VP stood his ground, staring across the lot toward his prey.

Evan studied the scene. Oddly, he smiled.

Patricia almost screamed. "You're *happy* about this?" she demanded. "I don't understand why you do this to yourself. What were you thinking?"

A hard look passed over Evan's face, and he kept his gaze focused on the school. "I was thinking I wanted my work shown. I painted it so that it would be seen, and now it's being seen. I don't care about the stupid festival. I only care that people see my work."

"That's great, Evan," Patricia said in an unnaturally high-pitched voice. Evan started to walk toward the front door, so she fell into step with him. "Do you know they're talking suspension—maybe even expulsion?" There was a slight waver in his step, but he continued on. "Is this really so important that you had to risk your future?"

Evan stopped abruptly. "My future?" he repeated, turning to face her. His green eyes flashed. "Forget the future. This is important to me *now*. This is important to *us* now. They can't control our creativity."

Patricia thought she saw doubt behind his defiant eyes.

"Evan, is this really about our freedom of expression, or is it about you throwing it in their faces?" she asked.

Evan took a step back, and she knew she'd struck a chord. Then he composed himself. He laid his hand on her shoulder and leveled her with a steady stare. "Patricia, sometimes you just have to take risks."

Then he turned and walked right up to the vice principal.

Patricia threw her arms up in helplessness. She was dating a maniac.

Stay cool. Stay cool. Stay cool. At least he'd handled that confrontation with Patricia without quivering and begging. And she hadn't tried to break up with him—actually, she'd run over to warn him. That had to mean she still cared about him, right? Evan smiled, letting out a deep breath.

After this whole mess was through, he was going to set things right with Patricia. Once and for all.

But he had some business to take care of first. Evan looked into Vice Principal Harris's smug face. *I'm going to throw up,* he thought. But he kept smiling and looked the guy right in the eyes.

"Morning, Mr. Harris," Evan said. "Seen any good art lately?"

Mr. Harris raised his chin, narrowing his impossibly tiny black eyes at Evan. "Shall we, Mr. Schnure?"

Harris said, placing a strong hand on the back of Evan's neck.

Evan shrugged him off, moving away slightly. "You can get sued for that, you know," he said. But his heart was hammering against his chest. Expulsion. Patricia had said expulsion.

Mr. Harris's amused expression fell away and was replaced by a near deadly glare. "Move."

Evan walked quickly up the steps and made his way through a crowd of whispering and cackling students. He pulled one of the doors open and strode through, not bothering to hold the door open for Harris. It almost slammed behind him, but Harris caught it at the last minute and walked in just as a few students in the lobby started to applaud.

"Speech!" someone yelled. The smattering of applause grew louder.

"Let's go!" Harris said.

Evan's eyes fell on his painting—still hanging on the center display. A few teachers were standing around, giving him stern looks. Even though his peers seemed impressed, the faculty obviously wasn't . . . and one important peer in particular was not pleased. Evan turned around and found Patricia in the crowd. She was standing just inside the lobby doors, her arms folded. She looked angry and disappointed.

Ouch. He'd known she'd be less than thrilled, but her expression stopped him cold. Evan fought back the nausea, promising himself he was going to work things out with her.

But he had to forget about Patricia for the moment and deal with the warden. Evan turned to face the hot seat—his pet name for the vice principal's office. The man even had a red chair for his interrogee.

Harris slammed the door behind him as Evan flung himself into the chair. He was so familiar with this particular piece of furniture that it practically molded to his butt when he sat down. Harris paced behind him like a caged lion. This was the period of silence intended to make Evan squirm. Instead he counted down in his head. *Five . . . four . . . three . . . two . . . one*—

"This one takes the cake, Mr. Schnure," Harris said, right on schedule. He walked around to the front of his desk, where Evan could see him, then leaned forward and pressed his fingertips against the desk's surface. "I think your career as a hood is finally over. You can't top deliberately going against a school-board ruling."

Hood? Who talked like that? "I guess not," Evan said.

"Did you think this stunt was funny?" Harris asked, staring him down.

Evan wanted to say that he didn't think any of this was the least bit funny. He wanted the chance to tell someone, anyone, even this flat-headed moron, his side of the story. That no one had told him there were rules. That this painting meant everything to him. That he just wanted someone to appreciate his feelings. But he couldn't say that, because it wouldn't matter. What he said never mattered to these people. They just rolled their eyes, said, "Troubled boy—so sad that he grew up without a father, but someone has to discipline him," and kept him after school. As if sitting inside for an hour in the afternoon was going to cure him of his principles. Adults could be such useless wastes of space.

"Are you going to answer me?" Harris demanded.

Evan shifted in his seat. "Whether or not I think this is funny, you already know what the punishment is going to be, so why don't you just tell me what it is and save us both some time?"

Harris's face turned red, and for a moment Evan thought the man's bad toupee was going to go up in smoke. But the vice principal turned his back to Evan, rubbed his face with his hands a few times, muttered something unintelligible, and turned back around. An eerie sort of calm had come over his features, making him look almost like a stone statue.

"I've already spoken with your mother. Two weeks' internal suspension and no school activities," he said calmly. "You may go to the detention hall now." He started to straighten some papers on his desk.

Evan's eyebrows shot up. "You mean I'm not expelled?" His voice sounded more grateful and psyched than he'd intended.

Mr. Harris continued to shuffle forms. "Trust me when I tell you, Mr. Schnure, that no one wants you roaming the streets. We're doing Jamesport a favor by keeping you in our sights."

Right, Evan thought. *Because I'm such a dangerous personality. I might break into people's houses and leave random pieces of art. Unbelievable.*

He stood up and lifted his bag. He tried to think of a good parting barb, but his mind was blank. He was just thankful he hadn't been expelled. His mom would have killed him. Evan opened the door to go.

"Oh, and Mr. Schnure," Harris said, looking up from his desk. "When I say no school activities, I mean no art club, no sporting events, no dance, no nothing. I want no disruptions."

Evan grinned. This was definitely a manageable punishment. He could manage without any school activities for a couple of weeks. "Thank you, Mr. Harris," Evan said. "Thank you very much!"

Mr. Harris shook his head in obvious bewilderment, and Evan walked out into the hallway. The place was deserted. Homeroom must have already started. Evan strolled down the center of the hallway toward the detention hall, wondering which unlucky teacher had the boring task of keeping an eye on the incarcerated this morning. It was Friday. That usually meant DeCaro had the first shift.

This was so great. Things were looking up, and Evan began to see everything in a new light. Sure, Patricia had been mad at him, but that was to be expected. She was the classic good girl. The important thing was, she'd been waiting for him. She'd tried to warn him. She'd cared enough to find him. And now he'd just stay in tomorrow and make sure Patricia's birthday painting was perfect and then—

Tomorrow. Evan stopped in his tracks, his stomach free-falling to the floor. Tomorrow was the dance, and Evan wasn't allowed to go. If there had been any grain of doubt that Patricia wouldn't go with Rider, it was gone now. Evan wasn't even an option. He couldn't even be there to keep an eye on them.

Rider was going to have the perfect chance to put the moves on Patricia. And there was nothing Evan could do about it.

"I heard he spent the whole day in detention hall," Max said, slamming his locker door shut. "I think that I would stab myself in the ear with a pencil out of boredom."

"At least he didn't get expelled," Isabel said.

"Where *is* he?" Patricia mumbled, standing on her tiptoes in an attempt to see down the hall over Max's head.

"Dude probably bailed," Lucas offered, coming up behind her. "After eight hours of solitary confinement the open road was most definitely calling his name." Lucas shrugged and sighed. "I'm just glad homey didn't turn me in."

Patricia turned to Lucas. "You were *in* on this?" she practically screeched.

Lucas, who was about twice her size, took a step

back and put up his hands defensively. "Chill, girl. It wasn't like I was going to be able to stop him, so I figured I might as well help."

"What were you thinking?" Patricia blurted out, smacking his arm.

"Ow. That's not cool," Lucas said with an injured expression. He rubbed his forearm.

Patricia backed off, rubbing her temples. "Sorry, Lucas," she said. "You're right. He would've done it anyway." She glanced at her watch. "If he's not here by now, he's not coming."

Isabel grabbed her bag. "Come on, let's go check out front. Maybe he's waiting for you in the parking lot."

"We'll come," Max offered, and the group started down the hall together.

Patricia's steps were heavy. She felt so bad for Evan. To be carted off like that in front of the whole school . . . Sure, some of the kids were clapping, but it still must have been humiliating. Harris had acted like he'd just snagged a serial killer.

She pushed open the lobby door and jogged down the steps.

"Where did he park?" Isabel asked, coming up next to her. Patricia studied the section of the parking lot in which she'd confronted Evan that morning. His moped wasn't there.

"He's gone," she said, not even bothering to hide the severe disappointment in her voice. "I can't believe he didn't even want to talk to me after being alone all day."

Isabel put her hand on Patricia's shoulder. "Don't worry about it, P. Lucas is right. He probably couldn't wait to get out of here. Just call him when you get home."

"Yeah, man. I'm always right," Lucas put in with a laugh.

Patricia nodded and tried to smile, but tears stung her eyes. Maybe he was mad at her about what she'd said that morning. But she didn't regret her words. He'd taken a major risk by going against the board's ruling, and it frustrated her to death that he never seemed to think of consequences.

A car screeched to a stop in front of them. "Hey, kids! Need a lift?" Courtney was grinning at them.

"Come on, Patricia," Isabel said. "The sooner you get home to call him, the sooner you'll feel better."

Patricia hoped she was right. "Okay. You guys coming?" she said to Max and Lucas.

"Nah. I got my ride," Lucas said, jangling his keys.

"I think I'll go with Luke," Max said. "We'll see you guys at the dance tomorrow, right?"

"Not me," Courtney said. "My date can't go."

Patricia froze. "What do you mean? Isn't Evan supposed to be your date?"

Courtney cut the engine and leaned farther out the window, resting her elbow on the frame. "Didn't you hear? I thought Evan would've told you."

Patricia gripped her binder to her chest and tried to swallow. "I haven't exactly seen him. What's going on?"

"He was banned from all school activities, including

137

the dance," Courtney said quietly. Patricia felt her face go white. "Sorry. I thought you knew."

"No. I didn't know," Patricia managed to say.

"That reeks," Lucas interjected.

"Seriously, man," Max said. "No Schnure? It'll be so lame."

Patricia's mind was in overdrive. So much for her plans to enjoy a night with her boyfriend. What had looked like a perfect weekend—dance, birthday, surprise party—was quickly turning into a bust.

"It's no big deal, though," Courtney said. "Aren't you going with Rider anyway?"

Patricia's head snapped up. "Who told you that?"

Courtney's face turned red, and she bit her lip. "Uh . . . Rider?"

"Well, you're misinformed," Patricia said. "I told Rider I was going to go with Evan, but it looks like that's not going to happen." Her voice steadily rose as she spoke.

"Hey! Don't shoot the messenger," Courtney said, starting her car again. "At least you can still have a date. I really think you should just go with Rider. Don't let Evan's burning need to be the rebel ruin your night."

Patricia grunted and walked around to the passenger seat of the car, climbing in. Isabel hopped into the backseat and waved good-bye to the guys.

"The only place I'm going is Evan's house," Patricia told Courtney, staring stonily through the windshield. "So you might as well start driving— and step on it."

TWELVE

EVAN OPENED THE front door of his house ever so quietly and closed it behind him with a soft click. A loud screech emitted from the general direction of the nursery. He'd never thought he'd be so happy to hear a Burko twin. If his mom didn't hear him come in, he could successfully avoid a major reaming for at least an hour. He rushed down the hall and ducked into his room. Safe.

"So you do exist."

Evan jumped out of his skin and reeled around. Patricia was sitting in his beanbag chair, looking quite comfortable.

"What're you doing here?" he blurted out, hugging his bag and his helmet. His whole body was tense. He didn't like being ambushed.

"Waiting for you," Patricia answered. "Where've you been?"

"Driving around. Did you sneak in the back door or something?"

Patricia stood up slowly and crossed the room, somehow avoiding tripping over his piles of junk without looking down. Her eyes were trained on his face. She reached over and pulled his stuff out of his hands. "Your mom let me in. I think she was hoping I'd be a good influence on you. Is that any way to greet someone you avoided all day?"

"What?" Evan asked. He sidestepped her and rushed over to pull up the covers on his bed. His room looked like the Tasmanian devil had paid him a visit. He sat down on top of his comforter. "I was in detention all day. How is that avoiding you?"

Patricia set his things down on his desk chair. "They had to let you go get lunch, but if they did, you were in and out in five seconds. And you could've waited for me after school."

"Patricia, I just wanted to get out of there," Evan said, his pulse racing. Was she going to break up with him right now? Here? In his very own room? How callous could she be? "So, what are you doing here anyway?"

Patricia crossed her arms over her chest. "I guess I just wanted to find out when you were going to tell me you weren't going to the dance."

Evan blinked. She sounded as if she was accusing him of something. That was rich—considering. "What does that have to do with anything? You already have a date."

Patricia's face flushed, but she didn't break eye

contact. "You know I didn't get matched up with anyone," she said. "I figured you and Courtney and I would all go together. I thought—"

"I found the pink slip in your backpack," Evan said, unable to listen to her lies. "I know you were matched with Rider."

Patricia opened her mouth to say something, but all she produced was a choking sound. She looked at the floor. The silence was so oppressive that Evan had to hold his breath.

Finally he spoke, his words cutting through the heavy air like a shot. "When were you going to tell me you were going with him?"

"I'm not going with him," Patricia said quietly, frozen in place.

"What?"

"I'm not going with him," she said, raising her face to look at him. Her blue eyes were swimming in tears and rimmed with red.

"Right. So why did you keep it a secret?" Evan demanded.

Patricia threw up her hands. "Because I knew how upset you'd get. And how did you find it anyway? Are you going through my stuff now?"

Evan couldn't believe it. What right did she have to get mad at him? He pushed his hands through his hair and laughed angrily. "Don't even try to turn this around on me. You're the one who lied."

This was torturous. He didn't want to argue with her anymore. He didn't want to see her cry or hear himself sounding insecure. He just wanted things to go back to the way they used to be. Why couldn't everything just be simple like it was a week ago?

"I lied so that you wouldn't get hurt," Patricia explained. "I didn't want you walking around thinking that Rider was my perfect match."

Evan's heart squeezed. He felt all the energy drain out of him. "Well, maybe he is," Evan said. *No, he isn't. Please say, "No, he isn't,"* he thought desperately.

But she didn't. She just stood there, staring at him with a stricken look on her face. And it was taking her far too long to process a reply.

So this was it. He'd been right all along. Patricia was ashamed of him. He was a screwup. Rider was a Mustang-driving, Polo-wearing, country-club card-holding, Matt Damon look-alike, and Evan was just a screwup. The prank he'd pulled today had obviously confirmed it for her. Patricia had finally woken up and noticed she was too good for him.

"What are you saying?" Patricia said finally. A single tear spilled over, rolled down her cheek, and hit her T-shirt, leaving a little expanding spot.

Deep breath. *Say it. Say it before she does.* "I'm saying maybe we should break up."

Patricia choked in an audible breath and looked away. Then she wiped beneath both eyes with a jerking motion and put her hand on the doorknob. Evan stared at her slim fingers around the brass fixture. *Don't let her go.*

"I can't take this anymore. You know what?

Fine," she told Evan. Her fierceness startled him. "If that's what you want—if that's all you have to say, then fine."

"Fine," Evan repeated. His mouth was working on its own as his heart screamed for him to grab her, hug her, and never let her leave. "Have fun with *Rider*." Damn. He sounded like such a bitter baby.

She nodded, slicing his heart in half. "Maybe I will." Then she was gone, leaving only the sound of the door slamming behind her.

"He doesn't care about me. He never cared about me!"

"Patricia, you know that's not true," Isabel reasoned. "That boy worships you. You're both just upset."

"Of course I'm upset!" Patricia fumed, flinging herself onto her bed so hard that Isabel bounced up from the force. "I just found out I wasted two whole months of my life on a guy who'll risk expulsion for a painting but balks the second he has a little competition in the love department." She took a deep breath. She was talking too fast and working overtime to keep from bursting into tears. It was an exhausting mix.

Isabel grabbed Patricia's wrists and pulled her up into a sitting position so that they were face-to-face. "Calm yourself and listen to me for five seconds," Isabel said. "It sounds to me like Evan is just insecure. And give me one good reason why he shouldn't be. Admit it—you've been flirting with the idea of going out with Rider."

Patricia rolled her eyes but couldn't keep her cheeks from blushing. "So what if I have?" she said. "I haven't *done* anything."

"Okay. Then why not?"

"Because I love Evan!" Patricia said, her voice cracking.

"Have you ever told him that?" Isabel asked.

"No," Patricia whimpered, standing up and shoving her hands in her pockets.

"Why not?"

"Because *he's* never told *me* that," Patricia answered, blinking back tears.

Isabel made a little exasperated sound. "Somebody's gotta say it first."

"I know that!" Patricia practically shouted. "But it's become increasingly obvious that he was never going to say it because he's practically forcing me to go out with another guy!"

"Patricia—," Isabel began.

"No. You know what? If he wants me to go to the dance with Rider, fine. I'm going." She picked up the phone.

Isabel grabbed her arm. "I really don't think you want to do that," she said seriously.

"Oh, I really think I do," Patricia said, dialing. She put the receiver to her ear, realizing that her whole body was trembling.

"Hello?"

"Hi, Rider. It's Patricia."

Isabel sighed and walked to the window, shaking her head. Patricia shot her an irritated glance, but it fell on Isabel's back.

"Hey!" Rider sounded extremely pleased. "I thought you might call."

Patricia almost asked him what he meant by that, but she didn't have time. She had to get this out. It was entirely possible he had already found another date and she was setting herself up for another rejection.

"Do you still want to go to the dance?" she asked, pressing her eyes shut.

"Sure," he responded. "What made you change your mind?"

Patricia relaxed her muscles and leaned back against her bed. She'd thought she'd feel relieved, but she just felt . . . empty. What should she answer? My boyfriend dumped me, so I'm all yours for the evening? "I just . . . well—"

"You know what? It doesn't matter. I'll pick you up tomorrow at eight. Sound good?"

"Sounds good," she replied, pressing her hand against her forehead. Nothing could possibly sound good at this moment. It was categorically impossible.

"Great. I'm glad you called. I knew you'd come around."

Patricia rolled her eyes. "Right, well, I'd better go," she said. "I'll see you tomorrow."

After Patricia hung up the phone, she pasted a smile on her face and turned to look at Isabel.

"It's all set!" Patricia said, feigning excitement. "This is gonna be great."

"Yeah, right," Isabel answered.

"What? Can't you even be happy for me?" Patricia asked. She turned her back on Isabel's skeptical face and opened the door to her closet.

"I can't be happy for you because you're ruining two of my best friends' lives," Isabel told her.

Patricia whirled around. "First of all, he broke up with me. And second, *I* am your best friend, not him. Whose side are you on?"

"I'm on your side," Isabel said calmly, picking up her purse. "It just happens to be the same side as Evan." Isabel gave her a pitying look. "I gotta go. I'm working tonight." She reached over and wrapped her arms around Patricia.

Patricia hugged her back and almost started to cry. Amazing how a simple hug could squeeze the tears out of her. "I'm sorry I yelled," Patricia said. "I guess I'm just a little freaked out."

"It's cool," Isabel said, flipping her long, curly hair over one shoulder. "I'll talk to you later."

Isabel walked out and closed the door behind her, and Patricia burst into tears. She let herself sob for a couple of minutes, not bothering to wipe away the tears. She finally caught her breath and straightened herself up.

Time to find something to wear tomorrow. Time to get psyched. Her stomach turned as she scanned her wardrobe. As if getting psyched were an option. She should just curl up in a ball, pop a sappy movie into her VCR, and bawl her eyes out.

Her eyes blurred, and she crumpled to the floor of her closet like a used tissue. Why had she told Rider she'd go? She couldn't go. Not like this. And she didn't foresee any vast improvements in the next twenty-four hours.

"Why, Evan?" Patricia whispered through her tears. "Why do you care more about a stupid painting than you do about me? Why didn't you care enough to fight for me?"

THIRTEEN

PATRICIA MOVED ACROSS the dance floor with the elegance of a princess, her head held high and her impossibly long, red dress trailing behind her like a peacock's tail. Her gleaming blue eyes were focused on Rider, and her placidly rapt expression illustrated the new and unexpected love she was feeling. He was hers. And she was happy.

"Patricia?"

She turned slowly, searching the crowded room for the source of the voice.

"Patricia. Don't."

Her beautiful features contorted with disgust and horror. She backed away, toward Rider, who put a protective arm around her shoulders and turned her away from the terrifying sight before her.

Evan looked down at himself. His clothes were torn and burned, and he was covered in a slick layer of green, smelly muck. Somehow he saw his face and realized with a sickening dose of dread that most of his teeth were missing and the ones that were still there either hung by a thread or were cracked and blackened. His hair was falling out in patches. Evan was petrified.

Rider huddled over Patricia and led her out of the room.

"Patricia!" Evan screamed. "Don't leave. Don't go with him!" But she didn't hear him. She was laughing now as Rider leaned in to kiss her.

Evan reached out to her, but she and Rider floated irretrievably into the distance. "No!"

Evan's eyes wrenched open, and it took him a good few seconds before he realized he was curled up in a ball on his bed, drenched in sweat. His heart pounded painfully. *It wasn't true,* he told himself. *Get a grip, Schnure. It was a dream.*

Evan sat up and pushed his damp curls off his forehead, then wrapped his arms around his bare chest. *It was only a dream.*

But suddenly the harsh reality of what had happened that day rushed upon Evan with a crushing weight. He had broken up with her. She was going to the dance with Rider. He had *told her* to go to the dance with Rider.

"What is wrong with me?" Evan said aloud.

He jumped out of bed, clicked on his halogen lamp, and covered his eyes when the painful light blinded him. He groped for the sweatshirt he kept on the back of his chair and pulled it on. He had to do something. He blinked a few times, squinting as he tested the glare. He finally found the clock. It was 3:42 A.M. Well, at least he'd have time to plan.

Evan sat down on the edge of his bed, put his elbows on his knees, and rested his head in his hands. Maybe he would just go over to her house in the morning and beg her to take him back—admit temporary insanity, and maybe all would be forgiven.

Only he knew it wouldn't be that simple. Evan sighed. He couldn't face another one of those long, tearful, completely frustrating conversations. There had to be another way.

Evan lifted his head and glanced around his room. He noticed in the mirror that he'd put his sweatshirt on inside out and backward. The Russell Athletic tag was curling up toward his neck. Evan was about to rip the tag off when he noticed something in the reflection off his right shoulder.

Patricia's painting.

Even though it wasn't quite finished, he'd brought it inside that morning to show his mother. He suddenly realized that Patricia might have even seen it that afternoon. But then, it didn't matter. Now she would never know it was for her.

Evan stood and picked up the painting. His heart tore as he studied the strokes, the palette, the composition. It was all for Patricia. And just as he'd poured his soul into his painting for the arts festival, he'd poured his heart into this seascape. He couldn't handle the thought that she might never see it. That she might never understand how much she meant to him.

Evan opened his bedroom door and tiptoed out into the carpeted hallway. He made his way through the darkened house toward the garage. He had to finish this painting. And he had to find a way to get it to Patricia.

Maybe there was still time.

"Honey! It's almost time!"

Patricia lifted her head from her hands and looked at the wall clock in the kitchen. It was 7:58. Her mother had been counting off the seconds until Rider arrived.

"Maybe *you* should go with him if you're so psyched," Patricia muttered, slumping over the counter.

"What was that, honey?" her mom asked cheerfully, popping her head into the kitchen from the living room.

Patricia stood up straight. "Nothing," she said.

Her mother's face was beaming with admiration and pride as she studied Patricia's outfit: short red dress, black strappy heels, Mom's diamond earrings that had been forced upon her the moment Patricia made the mistake of informing her mom she was going to the dance with Rider. "You look so beautiful, Patricia," her mom said.

"Funny," Patricia said wryly. "When I wore this dress to Courtney's birthday party and I was going with Evan, you tried to make me change for half an hour."

"Don't get smart," her mother said, half sternly. Apparently she couldn't quite manage to wipe the grin from her face, and it prevented her from being intimidating.

"Patricia! He's here!" her father shouted from the living room.

The butterflies in Patricia's stomach started to party. She rushed into the living room.

"Dad! What if he heard you?" she whispered.

Her father turned from his sentry position at the front window and quickly pinched her cheek. "He didn't hear me. Don't worry," he said in a goofy voice. Her mother giggled. Giggled! Patricia looked at them, sickened and bewildered. Who were these giddy people, and what had they done with her parents?

The doorbell rang, and Patricia suddenly had to pee. She told her parents to stall, and she made a run for the bathroom. Once safely inside, she braced her hands on the sides of the beige tile sink and stared at herself in the mirror.

"You can do this, Patricia," she told herself, breathing deeply. "It's one night. He's just a guy. Maybe you can convince him to bring you back early, and then you can just go to bed and wake up on your birthday."

Her birthday. Would Evan call? Would he stop by? Would he ever acknowledge her existence again? Why wasn't he here instead of Rider?

Patricia could hear her parents talking to Rider out in the living room. Her eyes had welled up with tears, but she willed them away, successfully avoiding a makeup disaster.

Might as well not torture Rider any longer. She realized she didn't have to go to the bathroom anymore. It must have just been nerves. She reached over and flushed the toilet for effect, then washed her hands and headed for the moment of truth.

As soon as she walked into the living room, Rider's eyes widened. Patricia blushed as she realized he was impressed by her appearance. And according to her sweaty palms and the sudden shiver she had to hide, she was just as affected by him. His bangs were pushed back off his face with a little bit of gel, making his blue eyes stand out even more against his tan skin. He was wearing pressed khakis that broke perfectly over his polished loafers, and his shoulders looked extra broad in his navy blue blazer.

"You look amazing," Rider said finally.

"Thanks," Patricia answered, clasping her hands behind her back nervously. "You too."

"Thanks." Rider glanced at her two grinning parents standing on either side of him, then walked between them to cross the room to Patricia.

He leaned over and kissed her quickly, softly, on the cheek, and Patricia's pulse raced. She felt his breath against her ear. The scent of his aftershave penetrated her senses and made her mind swim. She closed her eyes as the warming sensation of his closeness washed over her. "Whaddaya say we get outta here before your parents start talking about grandkids?" he whispered.

Patricia burst out laughing. Rider slid his hand down her arm and wrapped his fingers around hers. It felt right. Patricia pushed a nagging mental picture of Evan out of her mind.

She was barely aware of Rider saying good-bye to her parents, telling them he'd get her home before curfew. She couldn't think as Rider opened the front door for her and then rested his hand on the small of her back as they made their way to his car. Her mind was focused on repeating one simple thought.

Maybe Courtney was right. Maybe this was meant to be.

"She'll be there. She will. She'll be home in her room, talking to Courtney on the phone or watching *Sixteen Candles* for the nine-billionth time. She didn't go to the dance."

Evan kept his eyes focused on the road as he maneuvered his moped around a turn, attempting to delude himself the entire time. She had totally gone to the dance. She was there right now, hanging out with the seniors and cuddling in Rider's arms.

Evan's stomach clenched and he almost turned his bike back around, but he stayed on course. He had made a decision, and he was going to stick with it. If Patricia had decided to go out with Rider tonight, Evan was going to have to respect that decision. He was going to have to start acting mature at some point.

Evan pulled up in front of Patricia's house and

cut the engine. He glanced at her window and swore under his breath. The lights were out. No blue flicker from the television screen. She wasn't there.

His eyes traveled down to the front door. His original plan had been to walk up there and just knock on the door like a man—tell her parents he needed to see her and maybe even be polite about it. But now that he knew she wasn't there, his courage crumbled like a half-empty bag of potato chips.

Evan climbed off his bike and detached Patricia's painting from the rack on the back. He studied the tree that grew next to Patricia's bedroom window. Eminently climbable. He'd thought about this fact before but never had the chance to test it. Now seemed as good a time as any.

Evan shoved Patricia's painting under his arm, checked his back pocket to make sure the note he'd written her was still there, and then tiptoed across the lawn. When he got to the base of the tree, he reached out and touched the trunk. The first branch was at waist level, and other branches practically formed a winding staircase all the way up to Patricia's window. Cinch. Evan looked up into the blanket of leaves. Sure, climbing a tree one-handed and crawling into his ex-girlfriend's room in the black of night didn't quite fit with his new, adult outlook, but maybe sometimes there was just no room for maturity.

Gripping the painting as tightly as he could,

Evan started to climb. It was slow going, and every cracked twig and rustled leaf sounded like a blow horn to Evan's ears. Any minute now, Mr. Carpenter would come out with a shotgun and chase the interloper off his land. Evan's heart was in his throat as he continued to climb.

When he reached the window, he managed to sit down on a sturdy branch and stretch out his fingers toward the glass. If it was locked, he was toast. He pressed his palm against the flat surface and pushed up. Miraculously, the window moved. He tossed the painting inside, knowing it would land on Patricia's bed. After a quick pause to catch his breath and count his blessings, Evan gripped the sides of the window and pulled himself into Patricia's room, his stomach scraping along the bottom of the window and his legs kicking out behind him.

Evan tipped forward when his waist hit the ledge of the window, and he reached out and pressed his hand into the bed. Straining and grunting slightly, he started to pull his legs inside.

Then the light went on.

Evan tumbled into the room with a resounding thud and squeezed his eyes closed.

Busted.

FOURTEEN

"NO WAY, MAN! A full scholarship? That's *gotta* feel good," Rider said, slapping Jason Gertz on the back.

What would feel good, Patricia thought, *is you remembering I exist for five seconds.*

"So, when do you leave for preseason?" Rider asked, sipping his punch and gazing at Jason in awe. Patricia grabbed the blue ribbon attached to a helium balloon that was dangling in her face and started to shred it in an attempt to keep herself occupied.

"Day after graduation," Jason said, pausing in his face-stuffing marathon to answer through a mouthful of pretzels.

"That is so money, man," Rider said.

Patricia sighed and rolled her eyes. She let the balloon go and watched as the ribbon bounced in front of her face. She glanced around her immediate area, looking for someone, *anyone* to hold a semblance of a conversation with. Isabel and Courtney were no-shows—which probably meant they were setting up for the party she knew they were throwing her. That was great and all, but it didn't help her when she had no one to gossip with.

Patricia saw a few girls from the senior class glance in her direction. Patricia caught Meredith McMurray's eye and smiled. Meredith looked away. As Rider's date, Patricia had been getting the arctic treatment from senior girls all night—even from her friends from the team. And she thought seniors were supposed to be mature.

Patricia grabbed a Swedish meatball off a tray on the snack table and sucked it from the toothpick. She rolled the tiny piece of wood between her thumb and her forefinger and briefly considered stabbing herself in the eye with it to force a trip to the emergency room. It had to be more exciting than this. Maybe a Noah-Wyle-type resident would operate on her.

"Catch you later, man," she heard Rider say.

Finally! Rider stepped away from Jason and his entourage and reached behind his back for Patricia's hand. She glanced at his groping fingers and backed away. If he wasn't even going to bother looking at her, she certainly wasn't going to touch him. He was obviously scanning the room for the next person to schmooze.

It was unbelievable. Patricia had been nervous about hanging out with Rider because she was worried about being cool enough for a popular senior.

But all Rider cared about was working the room, kissing some butt. And it was actually quite pathetic.

"Rider?" Patricia said, rushing to get his attention before he set his sights on his next victim—though she didn't know who it could be. He'd already covered the student government, the cheerleaders, and the football team. "Are we gonna dance, ever?"

Rider grinned and placed his hands on her shoulders. "What's the rush? We have all night."

"We've been here for an hour," Patricia pointed out. All around her groups of kids were moving to the pulsing beat of the DJ's dance mix. They all seemed to be having such . . . what was the word again? *Fun.*

Rider laughed and brushed at his sleeve. "Don't whine, Patty; it doesn't suit you."

Patricia bit her tongue to keep from screaming. Suddenly Rider calling her Patty wasn't so cute. "I'm not whining," she said calmly. "I just—"

"Oh! Hey! Mr. Rosenberg!" Rider cut her off, calling to someone behind her. He patted Patricia's arm. "I'll be right back, 'kay?"

Patricia's mouth hung open as she turned to watch Rider jog across toward the far corner of the gym. He shook hands with an older man wearing a pair of small spectacles. A chaperon. Rider had deserted her to suck up to the *chaperons?*

This was just unacceptable. Concerned about looking uncool? Well, if being cool meant standing around watching the punch settle all night while Rider played Young Republican, she didn't want to be cool. She scanned the room, looking for a friendly face. Her eyes landed on Max and Lucas, who were grabbing attention in the center of the room. Surrounded by other sophomores, they were demonstrating some bizarre dance moves they'd probably picked up from the latest Puff Daddy video.

Patricia smiled and made a beeline for her friends. It was time to have a little fun—Patricia style.

From his prone position on the floor of Patricia's bedroom, Evan tried to squelch visions of Mr. Carpenter calling the police. Maybe Mrs. C. would appreciate the romanticism of his mission. He opened one eye, not sure which of Patricia's parents he should be hoping to see.

His gaze fell on two pairs of slim female legs. Courtney and Isabel were hovering over him. One smug, one shocked.

"Come here to trash the place, Ev? That's original," Courtney said.

Evan breathed a sigh of relief. There were no parental types in sight. "What're you guys doing here?" he asked, pushing himself off the floor.

"Setting up for Patricia's slumber party. What're you doing here?" Isabel demanded. She crossed her arms over her chest and leveled him with a stare. Evan noticed she had a roll of yellow streamers in her hand.

"That's tonight?" he asked. He slapped at his jeans and checked them for dirt, leaves, and rips. All seemed to be in order. "What about the dance?"

"We skipped it. Everyone's coming over after. We planned this thing before the dance was even thought up," Courtney answered, tossing a bag of balloons on the bed next to Evan's facedown painting. "Why am I even talking to you? I should've called the cops by now."

"Or at least Patricia's parents," Isabel pointed out. "This was one stupid move, Evan. I thought you were above this kind of thing."

"What kind of thing?" Evan demanded. They were both heading for the door. He lurched forward and grabbed each of them by the wrist. "You guys," he whispered hoarsely. "I'm only here to leave her a birthday present. I swear."

Courtney snatched her hand away. "Yeah, right," she said. "And tomorrow I'm giving all my clothes to charity and buying replacements at Kmart."

"No. Look." He reached over and grabbed the painting off the bed. He held it up for them to see. "Here. See? I'm not kidding. I just wanted to leave this for her and bail. I just wanted her to know that I . . . I mean, that I . . ."

"Evan! It's beautiful!" Isabel exclaimed. "She's going to die when she sees it. It's from the cove, right?" Isabel leaned in to study the painting.

Evan smiled and held it out to her. "Here," he said. "Take it over by the light."

Isabel carried the painting to Patricia's desk and trained the adjustable lamp on the canvas. Courtney joined her, bending over the painting and studying it with a stunned expression.

"I knew that was her favorite place, so I spent all this time there at different parts of the day; you know, so I could catch the right setting," Evan explained, leaning in behind them. "You really think it's good, Isabel?"

"Evan, it's unbelievable," Courtney said. She looked at him with admiration. At least he thought it was admiration. He'd never seen the expression on her face before, so he wasn't quite sure.

"Really?" he asked, stuffing his hands in his pockets. He was a tad uncomfortable receiving praise from his archenemy. "Uh . . . thanks."

"You must really . . . care about her," Courtney said, standing up straight and walking over to sit on the bed. "No one would ever do anything like that for me," she added.

"Seriously, Evan," Isabel said, handing the painting back to him. "Can I ask you a question?"

"Sure." Evan walked over to the head of the bed. He leaned the painting against the pillows, making sure it was right in the center.

"Why did you break up with her?"

Evan's shoulders knotted up, and he cringed. "It was a heat-of-the-moment thing," he told them. "I didn't want to do it. I thought she was gonna break up with me."

"Oh, that's good," Isabel said. "So, you wanted to beat her to it?"

"I didn't want to get dumped for that Rider jerk!" he said loudly. "You can't tell me she isn't interested in him."

"Girls? What's going on up there?" Mrs. Carpenter's voice called. Evan froze, and Courtney jumped up and bounded for the door.

"Nothing, Mrs. C.!" she yelled. "We're just trying out a . . . new CD!"

"Oh! Okay! Let me know if you need anything!"

Isabel tiptoed up to Evan and looked him directly in the eye. "Evan, Patricia is not interested in Rider. Trust me."

Right then Courtney started to cry. Evan glanced at Isabel, raising his eyebrows in a question. Isabel shrugged.

"You guys, I'm such a loser," Courtney said as tears coursed down her cheeks. "I messed everything up, and then you . . ." She flung her hand in Evan's direction. "You have to turn out to be sweet, and Patricia turns out to be smart, and I . . . I'm the bad guy!"

She buried her face in her hands.

"Courtney, you're rambling," Isabel said, obviously bewildered.

Courtney took a deep breath and lifted her head. Pieces of hair were stuck to the wet patches on her face. "Rider and I . . . we . . . uh . . . we set up the matches for the dance. Well . . . we set up one match."

"*What?*" Isabel and Evan said in unison. Evan was in front of her face in a flash. He wanted to reach out and shake her, which must have been evident because she backed away like a scared child.

"Courtney!" Evan placed his hands gently but firmly on her shoulders. "Explain this to me. Why would you set Patricia up with someone she doesn't even want?"

"Well, I didn't know she didn't like him. . . . I

mean . . . she *said* she didn't, but it was Rider. How was I supposed to believe her?"

Evan let her go and flung his hands in the air. "If I hear one more time about how perfect Rider is, I am going to self-destruct!" he said. He braced his arms on the top of Patricia's tall desk and tried to pull the emergency brake on his speeding brain. If Rider were here right now . . .

Courtney was talking again, preempting his revenge plans. "I thought it was so sweet and romantic when Rider asked me to help him," Courtney said in a somber, more subdued voice. Her tears were just trickling now. She sniffled loudly. "Of course, I didn't know at the time that he was gonna set me up with you as a joke."

"Do you realize . . . ," Evan began slowly, staring at a framed picture of himself that sat on Patricia's desk. "Do you realize that Rider's been manipulating Patricia from the beginning?" He turned to look at Courtney. "I mean, that whole shopping-for-decorations thing was a setup, right?" Courtney averted her gaze, which was a definite yes. "And then he probably did keep her out late on purpose so she would miss the board meeting, knowing it would make us fight and probably hoping it would break us up. But when that didn't work, he figured out a way to guarantee himself a date with her."

Evan paused, put his hands on his hips, and looked at the floor. He had a very strong urge to track Rider down and hit him. But what was even more disturbing was the fact that he was impressed. "The man is a genius," he said.

"A genius who's at the dance right now with the love of your life," Isabel pointed out.

Evan's head snapped up. "You're right," he said. "Enough of this sneaking around." He grabbed the painting off the bed and strode to the door. "Courtney, you run interference with the parents. Keep 'em away from the front door."

"What're you gonna do?" Courtney asked, wiping the tears from her cheeks.

"I'm going to the dance. I'm gonna go get my girl," he said.

"Oh, Evan," Isabel teased. "Fighting for your woman against all odds. Laughing in the face of authority. How very Harrison Ford."

Evan grinned. "What can I say? Even I must have some superhero in me."

The DJ grabbed his mike and jumped up on his plastic chair, a plastic lei swinging around his neck.

"This song's going out from Patricia Carpenter to all you conga maniacs out there! How you feelin'?"

As the opening trumpet blast of music blared from the speakers, Patricia grabbed Lucas and Max and a few others and started the obligatory conga line. At first the line was more like a tadpole than a snake, and Patricia almost gave up on the whole thing. But within minutes the line started to grow, and Patricia found herself goading people she didn't even know into joining as she wove her way around the room.

"Olé! Olé! Olé! Olé!" she sang at the top of her lungs. And the release sure felt good. Lucas, who was behind her and holding her waist lightly, joined in the song, adding a few extra *arriba*s as they went. Patricia was consumed by laughter. She immediately thought of Evan. If he were here, they would have been having this kind of fun hours ago.

As Patricia neared the gym door and started to plot her course to recross the room, she felt a hand close tightly around her biceps. Suddenly she was jerked aside.

"Ow!" Patricia glanced up at her captor. It was Rider. Why was she not surprised? She looked back at the conga line and noticed that Lucas was watching her with a concerned expression. She waved him on, then pried Rider's fingers from her arm and tossed his hand away.

"What do you think you're doing?" she asked, fuming.

"I was about to ask you the same thing."

Patricia reached up and pulled the tiny combs out of her hair, letting it fall over her shoulders. "I'm having fun for the first time all night, no thanks to you."

Rider smirked. "Yeah, well, you look like an idiot."

Patricia felt her face turn crimson, but she tossed her hair back and lifted her chin. "Excuse me while I take a moment to not care," she said.

"Oh, that's rich." Rider grabbed her wrist. "Come on, you're acting like a baby. Why don't you just have something to drink and cool off?"

Patricia was about to retort when a hand descended on Rider's shoulder from behind. Rider whirled around, and Patricia was shocked and more than a little bit psyched to see Evan standing there with a confident smirk on his face.

"What do you want?" Rider asked.

"Marshall, didn't anyone ever tell you that cheaters never prosper?" Evan asked coolly.

"Huh?"

Evan laughed and tilted back his head, then leveled Rider with a glare. "I know it's a hard concept, so let me put it in small words so that you can understand."

Rider clenched his fists at his sides, and Patricia's adrenaline surged. Evan was treading on thin ice. He leaned in toward Rider, who had a good four inches on him, and said, "I know you set yourself up with Patricia for the dance. And I know you've been trying to break us up ever since you got here. And personally, I don't care if you pummel my face into the gym floor right now because I know something that will make it all worthwhile."

Patricia's mind was reeling with an overload of information. It was all a setup. She didn't know how Evan had figured it out, but after seeing Rider's true colors, she believed it. Evan had been right all along. Rider was a total sneak.

"I know," Evan continued, looking around at the slight crowd his confrontation had drawn, "that you have so little self-confidence, you feel you have to plot and plan and scheme like some soap-opera villain to try to get a sophomore to date you. That's pretty sorry, man."

Rider finally found his voice. "*I'm* sorry?" he said. "I knew the moment I saw you, you little poseur, that Patricia was way too good for a loser like you. So I stepped in to show her what a real man looks like." He crossed his arms in front of his chest. "Besides, which one of us got dumped, and which one of us is gettin' some play tonight?"

Patricia felt her face go white. *Gettin' some play?* Was he serious? She saw Evan's hand ball up into a fist and held her breath as she waited for him to swing. But suddenly his fingers relaxed, and he took a deep breath.

"You know what?" Evan said smugly. "I'm not going to sink to your slimeball level."

At that moment Meredith McMurray walked by Patricia, holding a full glass of red punch with a lemon floating on top. Before Patricia even knew what she was doing, she'd grabbed the glass out of Meredith's hands and tapped Rider on the shoulder.

Rider turned to look at her. "Maybe he won't sink," Patricia told him. "But I will."

She flung the contents of the cup on the front of Rider's crisp white shirt before he even had a chance to flinch. The lemon stuck to his tie.

Evan let out a peal of laughter. Patricia handed the glass back to a stunned Meredith McMurray. "You want him? He's yours," she said.

Rider wiped his hands down the front of his

shirt, flinging the lemon on the floor. He stared daggers at Patricia. "You . . . little—"

Evan stepped in front of Rider. "I really don't think you want to finish that sentence."

A moment of intense tension passed as the testosterone flew between the two guys. Finally Meredith reached out and laid a hand on Rider's arm. "Come on, Rider," she said. "He's not worth it."

Rider blinked but didn't take his eyes off Evan's face. "Yeah," he said. "You're right." He let Meredith lead him away.

Evan grabbed Patricia up in a hug and spun her around, laughing in her ear. "That was so cool!" he cheered. "You are the best!"

Patricia's relieved laughter mixed with his.

"You want to get out of here?" Evan asked, holding her tightly.

"In the worst way," Patricia said with a smile. Evan replaced her on the ground, then took her hand and led her around a group of whispering freshmen.

Patricia started to giggle. The look on Rider's face had been classic. She was proud of Evan for not throwing a punch—no pun intended—but she was more proud of herself for putting that egotistical zero in his place.

For once in her life, she didn't mind being the center of attention.

FIFTEEN

"WOW! I MEAN . . . really, wow." Evan's words echoed in the empty school lobby. He stared at Patricia in awe. "That was possibly the best pitch I've ever seen you throw."

Patricia's laughter sounded like a song. She squeezed his hand and then twirled herself underneath his arm, cuddling into his side. "That *was* pretty cool, huh?"

"Another one for the yearbook," Evan answered, holding her close. They walked out into the moonlight, her body pressed up against his.

All Evan could think about was kissing this incredible, beautiful girl who was miraculously back in his arms. But he wasn't sure if he should. They were, after all, an ex-couple.

"What do I have to do around here to get a kiss?" Patricia asked as they reached the parking lot.

Evan's eyebrows shot up. "Hmmm . . . I don't

know. You could try soaking some raging egomaniac with punch." He smacked his forehead with the heel of his hand. "Wait a minute! You already did that."

Patricia giggled, and Evan leaned in for a kiss. But just as his lips were about to graze hers, a familiar voice made him jump.

"Aw! You guys are so cute!"

Courtney and Isabel were taking in the show from a few yards off.

"Hey, guys!" Patricia said. "What're you doing here? Shouldn't you be decorating my room or something?"

Isabel's face fell. "You knew?" Courtney screeched. "How did you know?" She stalked toward them. "You told her, didn't you, Evan? Admit it now and I'll spare you."

Patricia stepped protectively in front of Evan, laughing as she placed a hand on Courtney's shoulder. "Calm yourself, girl. I didn't know for sure until this very moment."

Courtney blinked. "You are such a weasel."

"All right! Break it up!" Isabel called, walking over to the little crowd. "Before we get back to . . . whatever it was we were doing, there's something our little manipulator here wants to say to you, Patricia."

Courtney cleared her throat and looked at Patricia. "I helped Rider set himself up with you for the dance," she said quickly, flinching as she spoke.

Patricia's mouth dropped open, but she didn't respond. The rest of Courtney's words came out in a rush. "And I never had an English test to study for, and I totally encouraged him to go for you, and you wouldn't even be here right now if it weren't for me, but now I know that Evan is way cooler than Rider, even if he is a little scrawny—"

"Hey!" Evan interjected.

"But the point is, I'm really sorry, and I'll never, ever butt in again." Courtney took a deep breath, closed her eyes, and crossed her fingers.

"Don't worry, Court. I'm not gonna bite," Patricia said lightly.

Courtney's eyes popped open. "So you're not mad?"

Patricia slung her arm around Courtney's shoulders. "Of course I'm mad. So this birthday party better be one kickin' affair and you'd better hope . . . no . . . pray that you aren't the first to fall asleep."

Courtney laughed nervously. "Isabel," she said. "Maybe we'd better go check on the food."

"Good idea," Isabel said, dragging Courtney by the sleeve toward her Land Rover. "You'll keep her occupied for a while, won't you, Evan?" she called over her shoulder.

Evan grinned. "If you'll do me the honor," he said, bowing slightly to Patricia.

She executed a small curtsy. "To the moped, good sir," she said.

Evan felt the tension around his heart ease as Patricia reached for his hand again. A breeze lifted the hair off her neck, and she closed her eyes, taking

172

a deep breath. Evan watched her serenely, feeling completely connected to Patricia for the first time in his life. It was as if everything that had happened in the past week had led up to this one moment of total love. They were together. And that was how it was meant to be. Evan was sure of it now.

Patricia opened her eyes, and Evan smiled. He saw the whole galaxy reflected in those eyes. "So, where to?" she asked.

"Come on," Evan whispered, tugging on her hand. "I have a little surprise."

The fear was totally exhilarating. Patricia clung to Evan's waist and clenched her eyes shut, even though she was already blindfolded by the red bandanna that Evan had tied on her in the parking lot. The chilly air whipped past her face, and she cuddled even closer into his back. Evan took a turn, and Patricia felt her knee come dangerously close to the ground.

"You're driving too fast!" she yelled.

"No, I'm not! It just feels that way because you're blind," Evan yelled back.

"Well, slow down anyway," Patricia called. But she knew he wouldn't, and she didn't care. The wind was pelting her face and knotting her hair, and she was loving every minute of it.

Suddenly the bike slowed, and Patricia jumped in her seat as Evan took them over a series of soft bumps.

We're at the beach, Patricia realized. She could

smell the salt air and feel the sand hitting her ankles, kicked up by the front wheel. A moment later she heard the surf pounding the shore, and she smiled to herself. Evan was such a hopeless romantic. All of that tough rebel stuff was just an act. He was the original softie.

"Everybody off!" Evan announced, pulling the moped to a stop. He slid from his seat, taking Patricia's hand. She was shaking as she shimmied off the bike, disoriented from the blindfold and still pounding all over from the thrilling ride.

"Hold on, I have to get something." Evan leaned over her and untied an object from the back of the bike.

"Don't worry. It's not like I can go anywhere like this," Patricia said, blinking against the soft cotton fabric of the bandanna.

Evan put one arm around her waist, and they started to walk. She tripped three times climbing over the dune that led to the beach, but she made it without falling on her face. Evan deposited her on a patch of cold sand.

"Ah! It's freezing!" Patricia exclaimed, wrapping her arms around herself.

"Sorry," Evan said, sitting next to her. "I wasn't planning on doing this tonight. I would've had a blanket."

Patricia cuddled in closer to him and nestled against his soft flannel. "This'll do."

Evan shifted and moved his arms around. Then she felt something press into the sand in front of her crossed legs. "You ready?" he asked.

"Are you kidding?"

"Okay. Take off the blindfold."

Patricia ripped the bandanna off her eyes.

Evan was holding a painting in front of her. It took a few blinks, however, to make out the scene. When it finally came into focus, Patricia caught her breath.

She glanced around to get her bearings and then looked back at the painting. "The cove," she whispered. "Evan, it's perfect." She reached out and lightly grazed the bumpy canvas with her fingertips. Every detail of the cove was represented, from the rocky jetty to the north, to the reeds that crowded the sand. But the painting was even more beautiful than the real thing. Evan had created a depth, a swirling display of color and grace that went beyond the simple cove she had always loved. It was as if he'd taken her special place and really molded it just for her.

"Evan, thank you so much," Patricia said, tears welling up in her eyes.

"Patricia, don't cry," he said, laying down the painting and touching his fingertips to her cheek. "It's just a painting."

"It's not just the painting." Patricia wrapped her hand around his wrist. "Thank you for everything. For . . . for caring enough about me to create something like this. For . . ." She swallowed, unsure if she would be able to say the words. "For finally fighting for me tonight."

"Was that what you thought?" Evan asked, his eyes glittery in the darkness. "That I didn't want to fight for you?"

Patricia dropped her eyes and nodded.

Evan took both her hands and squeezed. "I wanted to fight for you, Patricia. I wanted to so bad, but I didn't think it mattered. I'm just this loser who spends half his time staring at the ceiling of the detention hall. Who . . . who doesn't drive a Mustang and doesn't have a clue about clothes or style or girls—"

"Hey! That's my boyfriend you're talking about!" Patricia interrupted. She'd had no idea Evan was so down on himself. Whenever he stood up to teachers or hung out with their friends, he always seemed to have so much confidence. And he should—he was an incredible person. She picked up the painting and held it up for him. "I'd say you know *a lot* about girls."

Evan cracked a grin. "Well, maybe *one* girl."

"Oh, really? And who is this one girl?" Patricia asked. She placed the painting aside and wiggled across the sand and into his lap.

He hugged her tightly, holding her sideways so he could look at her. "Well, she has these incredible eyes and this amazing body—"

She slapped his stomach playfully, and he flinched but continued.

"And she takes risks when she thinks they're worth it, but she's not stupid about it like some people I know—"

She hit him again.

"And she throws a mean punch," Evan continued, laughing. Patricia giggled. Evan paused and took a deep breath. Patricia felt his chest rise against her, and he held the air for a moment.

Then he spoke. "And I love her . . . more than she could ever possibly understand."

Patricia clasped the fabric of his shirt. Every one of her senses was on alert. "Could you . . . um . . . could you say that again?" she asked weakly.

Evan leaned his face in closer to hers, and Patricia felt groggy and warm, as if she were being lulled through a sweet dream.

"I love you, Patricia," he said.

Patricia closed her eyes. Finally. "I love you too," she said.

Evan kissed her, wrapping her up in his warm, strong arms and cradling her neck with his hand. As she felt the strength of his emotions pour over her, she felt safe and happy and totally secure. The last week of their lives slipped away like a fading chord, lingering, then floating off into the realm of the ir-retrievable past.

Nothing mattered.

Nothing mattered at all but this moment. This kiss. This new world where there was just Evan.

Just her and Evan and the future.

Do you ever wonder about falling in love? About members of the opposite sex? Do you need a little friendly advice but have no one to turn to? Well, that's where we come in . . . Jenny and Jake. Send us those questions you're dying to ask, and we'll give you the straight scoop on life and love.

DEAR JAKE

Q: *There's this guy, Zach, who I used to pick on a lot and make fun of. He just got on my nerves. Well, now I kind of like him, and I'm not sure what to do. If I tell him, will he believe me after everything I've done to him in the past?*

KN, Hamilton, OH

A: Guys have an amazing capacity to believe that girls are interested in them even when there are absolutely no signs supporting their theories, so if you go so far as to *tell* him that you like him, there should be no problem. Of course, I'm not being totally serious here since the unstoppable male ego is certainly a common phenomenon, but not a universal one. Maybe Zach is one of those guys, like myself and a few others, who needs a little more reassurance of his irresistibility.

Either way, it can't hurt to try extra hard to share your feelings in an honest and straightforward way. Don't ignore the problem areas—that will just make things awkward. Acknowledge that you two didn't get off to the greatest start, and apologize for treating him the way you did. Then let him know that you're ready to move on from there, and find out if he feels the same way.

Q: *I'm still pretty good friends with my ex-boyfriend, Jason, so we hang out sometimes. A couple of weeks ago we ended up in a big crowd that included my current boyfriend, Paul. I was worried things might be awkward between them, but it was just the opposite—Jason and Paul got along really well. Now they're actually becoming friends, and they even went to a basketball game together, without me! Is this incredibly bizarre? How should I react?*

ES, Mahwah, NJ

A: It does sound rather unbelievable that the two guys could bond so easily when the one major thing they have in common (you!) should—if anything—cause serious tension. But I have seen it happen. In fact, Barry, one of my good friends now, is a guy I met through a girl (what was her name again?) that I dated a long time ago.

In a way, it makes a kind of sick sense. Jason and Paul each had qualities that appealed to you, and these are probably the same qualities that they like about each other. Since you and Jason are still friends, I assume that you're both okay with the fact that the romantic thing is kaput. Therefore Jason and Paul's friendship doesn't have to be as sticky for you as it might seem. However, stress to each of them that you want their respective relationships with you to be kept private. And if it starts to get out of hand and you're feeling very uncomfortable or left out, talk to Paul.

DEAR JENNY

Q: *My boyfriend and I have been planning on going to the prom together for the whole year because we've been a couple since sophomore year. But we broke up a week ago, and the prom is at the end of the month! All the reservations are made and everything. Do we still go together or find new dates or what?*

RK, Napa, CA

A: That is the worst feeling, isn't it? Believe me— I've been there. My boyfriend of three years broke up with me a couple of weeks before my older sister's wedding. Not only did I still have to look happy for the big event (thank goodness for expert eye makeup!), but I had to scramble for an escort at the last second.

I know it might seem like an easy out to go ahead and attend the prom with your ex. After all, you're used to him, everybody *expects* you two to come together, all of your friends have plans depending on your coupleness, yada yada yada. But if you want the truth, going with him will only remind you of what you used to have—but don't anymore. My advice? Go with a good friend who's guaranteed to make you spend the whole night laughing and having a blast. My sister's wedding album is full of pictures of me and my buddy Chris goofing around, being silly, and—most important—smiling.

Q: *Jon and I have been doing some serious flirting lately, but neither of us has come out and said we're interested or anything. I* was thinking of sending him some flowers from a "secret admirer" and then seeing how he reacts. Is that a good idea or totally stupid?

RN, Fenton, MO

A: I like the way you think—sly and sweet are a great combination. But you're also cautious, which is equally important because risky moves like this are a pretty big gamble. First off, he might not realize the flowers are from you. He could be confused or maybe become intrigued by the thought that the quiet but stunning girl in his math class who he's never exchanged a word with is after him big time.

On the other hand, even if he does guess his admirer correctly, it's possible that he'll think you're coming on a little strong. The best thing you can do at this point is to continue flirting and try to up the level of intensity slowly so that you can judge his reaction and figure out if he thinks this is going in the direction you're hoping it is.

Do you have questions about love? Write to:
Jenny Burgess or Jake Korman
c/o 17th Street Productions,
a division of Daniel Weiss Associates
33 West 17th Street
New York, NY 10011

Don't miss any of the books in *Love Stories*
—the romantic series from Bantam Books!

SUPER EDITIONS

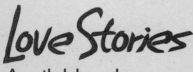

BFYR 232